I0757763

# Bound by Danger

UNDERCOVER MAGIC BOOK SIX

ISBN: 978-1-951738-33-4 (Paperback Edition)



Cover Design by CReya-tive Book Design

Edited by Mo Sytsma of Comma Sutra Editorial

Proofread by Dominique Laura

*For Kim, the sister of my soul,*
*You are juuuuuust right.*
*Thank you for loving Quinley. You're the reason this book exists.*

"Love can do more than break your heart. It can shatter your mind."

— O'BENGH

# CHAPTER ONE
## QUINN

For as long as Quinn Satori could remember, she'd been haunted by memories that were not her own. As an Animagi memory weaver with perfect recall, her mind was a steel trap when it came to retaining information. Which was why silence—blissful, perfect silence—had always been a welcome friend.

Until today.

Never in her life had silence been so unsettling.

Even though she was not alone, the oppressive hush in Nathaniel Cohen's office was worse than a tomb. Despite being poshly furnished, the acting Director's designated room lacked warmth, along with any personal details as to the man it belonged to. It may as well have been empty for all she could glean from it.

Quinn couldn't remember the last time she hadn't been able to sniff out some sort of clue about the person a space belonged to—which meant it had never happened before.

But she knew that had nothing to do with the unease prickling beneath her skin.

They'd been summoned to help the Guardian solve a case. Since the Brotherhood was comprised of highly skilled immortal warriors who were the absolute best of the best, being called in to assist was not a compliment. It was a Hail Mary.

If the Brotherhood had to resort to asking for help, something was very, very wrong. Like 'life as we know it could cease to exist' wrong.

In layman's terms, supernatural fuckery was afoot.

Fuckery that had absolutely nothing to do with her.

Quinn shifted in her seat, crossing and uncrossing her legs, adjusting her skirt, sighing heavily. She didn't want to be here. She was done fighting other people's battles. They'd just won a damned war, for fuck's sake. Didn't that earn her a vacation?

The way she saw it, she and Finley should be on a beach somewhere, sipping umbrella drinks, wearing little more than sunscreen and their smiles. Or, better yet, they'd be holed up in his newly restored penthouse with him balls deep inside her.

Now *that* would be a proper celebration. Because after months of her self-imposed celibacy, she was beyond ready for it to end. She'd made herself a promise: if they defeated Mikel, she would finally admit to her feelings for her British Man of Mystery and let him fuck her stupid. It was a promise she had every intention of keeping, starting—she checked her watch—four hours ago.

Quinn let out a little growl of frustration. Whatever reason Nate had for being late to his own damned meeting better be end of the world level important because that was about the only justification she'd accept for not being underneath—or on top of—her sexy-assin Guardian right now.

At least, she thought he was hers.

Other than a few stolen kisses and impassioned words, they hadn't exactly had a chance to hash out all the details of their relationship. There hadn't been time between nearly dying and dealing with the fallout of a madman's war.

She'd denied herself for months. Years, even. Tonight was supposed to be about the two of them finally sealing the deal.

Instead, they were here. Waiting. No closer to falling into bed with each other than they had been before returning from Novasgard.

And it was driving her insane.

Quinn snuck a glance at Finley. He didn't seem to share her impatience. He sat beside her, looking delicious in his tailored gray suit. With his head propped against his fist, hazel eyes with their silver flecks trained on her, and a small, knowing smile curving his full lips.

*The ass.*

He was enjoying this, watching her squirm and likely knowing the exact reason.

She huffed and looked away, pretending not to hear his low chuckle.

Until the phone call a few hours ago that had shot her plans for an epic fuck fest straight to hell, Finley had been on administrative leave pending a full investigation for the role he played in ousting the prior Director. The Guardians were notorious for following protocol. They might lead the game when it came to warfare and strategy, but their stubborn insistence on adhering to centuries-old bureaucracy meant anything requiring paperwork went painfully slow. Whatever happened must have been beyond serious for Nate to reinstate Finley out of the blue.

And that, she realized, was the real reason she couldn't shake the sense of foreboding that had settled deep into her bones.

After everything they'd already sacrificed, danger still lurked in the shadows, hunting them. She almost lost him once. Could still smell the tang of his blood pooling onto the wet asphalt and feel her heart seizing in her chest as she clung to his unmoving body. She'd barely survived losing him once.

She wouldn't be so lucky a second time. Not when she could recount the first with perfect clarity every time she closed her eyes. A woman could only take so much when it came to the man she . . .

"What's taking him so long?" Quinn snapped when the silence and her tumultuous emotions became unbearable.

Finley smirked, one dark brow lifting. "In a hurry, Satori?"

Despite the panic clawing at her chest, Quinn adopted her patented, breezy tone. "I have places to be . . . people to do."

His gaze went molten. "By people, you better be referring to me, princess. We have an understanding."

"Do we?"

*Ah, yes. This was much better.* She'd never admit it out loud, but their flirtatious banter had been one of the few things keeping her going during the hell of the last few months. It was her reprieve, her safe place. Okay, fine. *He* was her safe place.

A little sexy small talk was exactly what she needed to stave off the full-blown panic attack threatening to consume her at the thought of something else happening to him.

Finley leaned forward, grabbing her chair and dragging it closer until their knees brushed against each other, forcing her thoughts to scatter and her focus to lock onto him.

Only him.

God, she loved it when he did that. There'd never been anyone else in her entire life who could make her brain shut the fuck up the way he could. The way he *demanded.*

"Just because our business remains unfinished, Satori, doesn't mean you're a free woman. You belong to me, Quinn."

Her heart fluttered at the words, and she barely maintained her aloof tone. "Is that so?"

He reached out, running the tips of his fingers down her cheek and causing her breath to stutter. "Your body betrays you, love. But I'll take the bait." His lips curled in a slow, seductive smile. "Allow me to prove it to you."

"How do you propose to do that?"

He lifted a single shoulder in a shrug. "Just a simple demonstration. A promise of what's to come once we're finished here."

The words confirmed he had, in fact, known the reason for her restlessness. Or at least part of it. Delivered in his sensual growl, they had the added effect of sending a bolt of lust slamming into her. A dull throb pulsed between her legs, the echo of her racing heart. She swallowed.

"A demonstration? Here?"

He gripped her chin lightly, leaning close until the mint and clove scent of him consumed her. His words were playful, though his gaze was anything but. The intensity she found there seared her, sending arousal zinging through her body.

"Wherever I say, whenever I say. That's how this is going to work, princess." He shifted, his mouth all but touching hers. "Now . . . take off your knickers."

Her body's reaction was instant. Her nipples pebbled beneath the silk of her camisole. Her core tightened, and that dull throb transformed into a full-body tingle. For a second, her mind went utterly and blissfully blank. Then her brain caught up with her. She wanted to obey, to give in to his every demand, but curiosity had always been her downfall. She couldn't resist the temptation to push back, to find out how he'd respond to her small act of defiance.

She dropped her voice, matching his low, seductive tone. "What makes you think I'm wearing any?"

His lips quirked up in a knowing smirk. "Prove it."

God. The things that did to her. She wanted to crawl into his lap then and there. Quinn only just managed to check the impulse, enjoying their game too much to give it up that easily. Especially when it gave her something else to focus on.

"You want me to *prove* I'm not wearing any underwear?"

"That's right, love. Lift that skirt of yours, spread your legs, and show me."

Her breath hitched. Fuck, this was hot. And besides the fingers holding her chin, he wasn't even touching her. If it was this good already, she knew she'd probably combust when she got all of him. She couldn't help but wonder just how far he intended to take this.

"Now, princess."

Heart racing, Quinn sat back in her chair, a pang of disappointment at losing his touch underscoring her rampant lust. She slid up the sides of her skirt, just enough that she'd be able to follow his next order, aware with every wild beat of her heart that the door could open at any moment and Nate could walk in.

As she parted her knees, Finley's gaze traveled down her body, a muscle in his jaw ticking when he noticed her nipples straining against her shirt. And then lower, his head tipping slowly down so he could see what she had on beneath her skirt.

She could feel his gaze moving over her like a physical caress. Her body was hot, achy. She'd never been this turned on by something as simple as a few filthy words and some heated looks. But then . . . she'd never had Fin. Not like this. Not completely. And he was power and dominance and sex all wrapped up in one delicious package.

Better still, he was hers . . . or he was about to be. Just as soon as they finished up this fucking meeting.

"Naughty minx. You lied."

Quinn's laugh was just this side of breathless. "Oops."

"Take them off, Satori. They belong to me."

She cast a furtive look at the door.

"Don't worry about him. It's my job to worry. It's yours to obey. Now take them off, or I'll bend you over my knee and do it for you."

Quinn almost whimpered. The thought alone was enough to make her hesitate. She liked option two. A whole fucking lot. Clearing her throat slightly, she forced herself out of her chair, hooking her fingers beneath the scraps of lace and silk, and tugged it down. She was all too aware of the brush of her skirt against her bare skin and the cool air over her desire-heated flesh. She was so turned on it was bordering on painful. Her skin was hot, each scrape of the fabric a reminder that it wasn't the touch she craved. She wanted more. *Needed* more.

Once she'd tugged the lingerie to her knees, she was leaning forward enough that her shirt gaped, and Finley made no efforts to hide the fact he was blatantly staring.

*What's good for the goose . . .* Quinn let her eyes drop to his lap, a soft gasp escaping at the thick bulge in his pants.

Jesus. It was hot, so hot, seeing how turned on he was by the simple act of her undressing. No. That wasn't it. He was turned on by her obedience. Fuck, so was she. She was practically high with it. There was something incredibly freeing in doing what she'd been told, allowing her mind to empty of everything except for him.

For a second, she wondered if he knew that taking charge of her this way was akin to him coming to her rescue, of saving her from the nightmares haunting her every waking thought. But then she caught that heated look in his eyes again and hastened to obey. What did it matter if he knew, so long as it was true?

She pulled her panties down the rest of the way, hooking one finger through the fabric and offering it to him as she straightened.

Finley reached forward to claim the damp piece of lace, but she tugged her hand away.

"I want those back when you're done with whatever game you're playing."

"Never gonna happen," he said, snatching them from her. Then he sat back in his chair, his eyes never leaving hers.

"What now?" she asked, her voice betraying her need.

He raised his brow, held her panties up to his nose, and inhaled. His eyes closed, and he let out a deep, pleasure-filled rumble. "Delicious."

Quinn had to clench her thighs together to prevent the proof of her arousal from dripping down her legs.

After a second, he pinned her with his hazel gaze. "Now, princess, you're going to sit down and suffer through this meeting with me."

"What?" she snapped, the sudden shift feeling like ice water dumped straight over her head. "Th-that's it? You're just going to leave me like this?"

He smiled, and it was so filled with carnal promise that she whimpered. He leaned forward, his eyes pinned on hers, his voice barely above a whisper. "I want you to sit there, aware of your dripping cunt and how badly it aches for me. I want you desperate and needy and ready for everything I have planned for you once we get home."

Quinn forgot how to breathe, her next words sounding thin even to her own ears. "Why wait?"

His grin stretched. "We have a meeting to attend."

"You sonofabitch."

"Bastard is more appropriate. But be a good girl, princess, and I'll give you everything you could ever want."

Her eyes dropped meaningfully to his lap. "Right now there's only one thing I want."

Finley chuckled. She never knew a man's laugh could sound so fucking sexy, but that husky rasp was just as potent as his gaze. Her body responded as if he'd touched her.

"Consider my cock your reward," he said, sitting back and propping his ankle on his knee. "If I recall correctly, I believe that's what you refer to as motivation."

"I—"

The door clicked open. Quinn's eyes flew wide, and she sat down gracelessly, giving the sides of her skirt a tug in a desperate attempt to pull the fabric down to a more appropriate length. Her heart lurched in relief when she spotted Finley tucking her pilfered panties into his suit jacket.

His eyes twinkled and he winked at her, a small smirk playing about his lips. "To be continued," he mouthed as Nate strolled into the room.

# CHAPTER TWO

## QUINN

It was a testament to her control that she managed to level a look dripping with cool annoyance at Nate while her heartbeat thundered in her ears and her pussy throbbed with need.

Beside her, Finley was the picture of casual male elegance. If she hadn't known to look for it, she wouldn't have noticed the slight bulge in his breast pocket or the way he subtly ran his hand down his lapel, lingering just a hair longer over the lump.

*Fucking clit tease.*

Quinn shot him what she considered a level-two death glare. Not enough to eviscerate him on the spot, but leaving him with no doubt that he was in for a world of hurt.

*Two can play this game, Batman. You have no idea what fresh blue ball hell you've just unleashed.*

Finley knew her too well to miss the message. He couldn't read her thoughts outright, but she was certain he guessed them easily enough based on their past exchanges. So she continued to glare at him until he ducked his head, hiding his smile as Nate made his way over to them.

The Guardian took a few steps, stopped, risked a glance between the two of them, and then wisely chose not to comment on the blatant sexual tension permeating his office.

"Sorry to keep you waiting," he said, heading for the padded leather chair behind his massive oak desk. "The debrief from Simmons ran long."

"Not a problem," Finley answered.

But Quinn had no intention of letting the acting Director off that easily. Lifting her chin, she snapped, "It's categorically rude to call an emergency meeting and then be late. You could have at least provided us with an update so we weren't sitting in here with our thumbs up our asses while you were off wasting our time."

Nate froze in the act of unbuttoning his suit jacket, his warm brown gaze darting between them once more. "Uh . . ."

Quinn narrowed her eyes, suspicion taking root as she turned to stare at her sexy Brit, who was pointedly refusing to look at her.

Suspicion turned into cold hard fact.

*That scheming crumpet muncher.*

The Guardian *had* sent word—to Finley—and the dick whistle hadn't breathed a word of it to her. Stupid telepathic bond. They'd probably been in communication ever since she and Fin set foot in the building. Which meant he'd known exactly where the other man had been the entire time and that she'd never been in any danger of getting caught with her skirt up.

His whole 'it's my job to worry' speech had been a sham. She was oddly disappointed by the realization. The threat of being discovered had been part of the excitement. He'd known it and tricked her, using her impatience and hunger for him as fuel for his little game. A game she'd wholeheartedly approved of, right until its anticlimactic end.

The whole thing had been a complete and total mind fuck.

Quinn couldn't decide if she was impressed or pissed off. The fact that he pulled it off spoke to how well he already knew her and anticipated her needs. Generally, she didn't appreciate being toyed with. But this was Finley. The rules were different with him.

They always had been.

Since she could hardly unload on him in the middle of the Brotherhood's headquarters, no matter how much he deserved it, she channeled her sexual frustration into something more practical. Like a scathing, sharp-edged temper which she then unleashed on the only other person around.

"Do better next time," she snapped at Nate as she crossed her arms over her chest. "We're doing you a favor by even being here. The least you can do is make a point of being punctual."

To his credit, Nate looked appropriately chastised as he sat down. "You're right, of course. My apologies, Ms. Satori. It won't happen again."

Quinn thawed a little. She appreciated a man who knew how to grovel. "You may as well call me Quinn. No need for us to stand on ceremony."

He tossed her a relieved smile, likely taking her permission to call her by her first name as a good sign regarding her willingness to help with his request. What he didn't realize was she hadn't decided one way or the other. She wasn't a consultant and her services weren't for hire, but he was Finley's friend, and he'd made things easier for them when he could have easily done otherwise. While that hadn't earned him her loyalty exactly, it did mean she'd at least listen before making up her mind.

She could feel Finley's gaze on her, but now it was her turn to refuse to look at him. He thought he was so cute, tricking her out of her underwear. Well, the joke was on him. Only the two of them knew she was sitting here ruining her Prada skirt. But when they eventually stood up, there'd be no missing what was going on beneath his slacks.

The thought made her feel oddly vindicated, though there was no getting around the low hum of arousal still lingering under her skin. They needed to get this meeting over with before she started rubbing herself against the chair in an unconscious attempt to get some relief.

Giving herself a mental shake, Quinn refocused on Nate as he grimaced and pushed a small rectangular card into the center of his desk with the tip of his fountain pen.

There was some kind of inscription on the shiny black surface, but she couldn't quite make it out from where she was sitting. Leaning forward, both she and Finley reached for the card at the same time. Nate visibly tensed when their fingers brushed over its metallic face. As her fingertips made contact, a tiny zap of magical energy raced up her arm. Beside her, Finley let out a low hiss.

Nate shook his head. "Haven't the two of you learned by now not to touch something before you know what it is?"

Quinn and Finley let out embarrassed chuckles as they leaned back in their chairs.

"Sorry, I wasn't expecting it to be warded," she murmured. "I've always been a curious cat, and it *is* in a sphinx's nature to solve riddles. Speaking of, why did you call us here?"

Nate's demeanor changed at the question. He let out a heavy sigh, his shoulders drooping. "There was an accident. One of ours answered a call without waiting for backup. He's trapped, and we need the two of you to go save him."

Quinn glanced between the two Guardians, feeling like she was missing something. "I don't see how I'm supposed to help you. Maybe you have us Animagi confused, but Lina is the one who modifies reality. I'm only good with memory problems."

"Don't sell yourself short," Finley said. "You and I both know how powerful the mind can be. Often what people believe to be true is far more real and terrifying than what they experience in the outside world."

Quinn bit back a smile. She'd had the same argument with Lina countless times. Usually, while debating which one of them had the more impressive gift. She'd never actually force him to declare a winner, but it was nice to know which side of the debate Finley was on.

Nate sat forward and clasped his hands in front of him, deep lines bracketing his mouth. "There's no mistake, Miss—Quinn—you're exactly who we need. You and Finley both."

The mention of his name made Finley sit up straighter. "What kind of trap did Marquez set off?"

"We're not entirely sure. None of us have been able to breach his mental walls to find out."

"Mental walls?" Finley repeated. "You mean he's—"

Nate nodded before Finley finished speaking. "It's the damnedest thing, but yes, he's imprisoned in his mind. I've never seen anything like it. We know he's in there; the caster made no effort to conceal his handiwork, so there's magical residue all over him. He reeks of it, but we can't reach him. He's too far gone."

"And you think one of us can?" Quinn asked, still unsure what part he expected her to play.

"If I connect your minds, link them the way all Guardians are linked, I believe the two of you, together, might be strong enough to break through the spell."

Quinn's back snapped ramrod straight. "You want to *what?*"

The man already lived in her mind rent-free. She didn't need to hand over the keys to the entire fucking castle and grant him full access to the rest of her. Some thoughts—some memories—belonged to her alone.

"It's not as invasive as it sounds," Finley said in a low voice, correctly interpreting her fear. "Through the bond, we'll be able to stay in contact. It's easy to lose yourself when you go that deep into someone else's subconscious. The connection will prevent either of us from getting lost. Think of it like an anchor."

"I guess that doesn't sound so bad. Will it be permanent?"

"Only if you want it to be," Nate assured her.

She pursed her lips, something still not adding up. "If it's that easy, why ask us? This guy's on your naughty list, and I'm not even part of your boys' club. I mean, if you want to get technical about it, I'm the new head bitch in charge of what's left of the Mobius Council —a group that, last I checked, your not-so-secret agency considered public enemy number one. Surely there are a couple other strapping young lads lying around eager to prove themselves. Why not ask them?"

Finley disguised his laugh as a cough while humor lit up Nate's eyes.

"I'm sure there are, but you are the two strongest telepaths we currently have access to. The previous Director"—his amusement transformed into disgust at the memory of his predecessor—"wasn't very *encouraging* when it came to our men perfecting that gift."

"He wanted to make sure no one was ever as powerful as him," Quinn guessed.

"Exactly."

"I should have done more than steal his memories," she grumbled.

Finley reached out and covered her balled-up fist with his warm palm. "Trust me, it was the perfect punishment."

"I'm going to level with you, Quinn, because I'd be lying if I said there wasn't any risk. I wouldn't put this on you if there were any other option. It's not the kind of responsibility to lay on a civilian, but frankly, you're our only hope. You are uniquely suited to this task in ways the Brotherhood doesn't come close. With your gifts of modification and compulsion, I think you might be the only person alive capable of untangling Marquez from his prison. I don't know exactly what you're going to face in there, but I can only assume it's some pretty intense magic. I want to send in one of our own with you—someone you trust—because I want you to feel safe and have a ripcord to use if you need it. Usually I'd never risk someone outside our ranks, but we've only got one shot at this, so I need to stack the deck. That means sending in the best. And you, Quinn, are the best."

She released a heavy sigh, already knowing this wasn't something she'd be able to refuse. Despite her prickly exterior, she didn't like the idea of anyone suffering when there was something she could do to help.

"Flattery will get you everywhere, Mr. Cohen."

"I thought we weren't being formal, Ms. Satori," he said, tossing her his most charming boy-next-door smile.

Before she could respond, Finley's hand squeezed hers, warning her to stop flirting. At least, that's what she assumed it meant until he bit out, "I will not allow you to coerce her into this, Cohen."

"It's the truth."

"Her life is worth more than a hundred of ours."

Nate's expression went slack, and then something like clarity flashed in his eyes. His voice was filled with jealous wonder when he spoke again. "You found your purpose." His eyes flicked to her. "She's yours."

Quinn's chest hollowed out, her heart stopping entirely before jerking back into action. Lina had explained what that meant to her. How Guardians were taught they'd been created to serve one true purpose. If what Nate claimed was true, then she and Finley were . . . fated. Meant to find one another across all space and time. Quite literally made for each other.

While not always romantic, the bond between a Guardian and his charge was said to supersede all others in importance. And once the vow was given, it lasted a lifetime. Nothing, save death, would ever come between them.

For Nord and Lina, it had been instant. He'd made his vow to her that first night. But Finley . . . She bit her lip, turning to face him.

*Had he known? And if so, for how long? Why is this the first I'm hearing about it?*

Finley's expression was stony and closed off, a muscle ticking in his jaw. He glared at Nate, his gaze fierce as he said, "I've made no vow."

"Doesn't make it any less true, you lucky bastard."

"You're asking me to put her life at risk for no damn good reason—"

"I'm asking you to go in with her and ensure that if things go sideways, you both get out. Is there anyone you trust more to protect her than yourself?"

"Of course not."

"Then I'm not seeing a problem."

Finley let out a humorless chuckle. "You wouldn't."

Realizing this would only continue unless she intervened, Quinn interrupted, "If I'm really the only one who can do this, then the choice is mine alone."

"Quinn—" Finley's gaze was conflicted.

"No," she said, pointing at him, "you're in enough trouble right now. I'll deal with you and the secrets you've been keeping later. As for you," she said, turning her attention back to Nate, who was currently trying to conceal an amused smirk behind his hand. "I have one more question."

"Shoot."

"How long has he been trapped?"

"A couple of days."

She bit her lip. As far as news went, it wasn't of the good variety. In fact, it was very solidly in the bad category. The mind eroded when it was disconnected from reality. If Marquez stayed untethered much longer, even she may not be able to reach him. They were officially on borrowed time.

"So let me just make sure I understand. Basically, you're asking us to jailbreak a man out of his own mind, potentially against his will?"

"Essentially . . . yes."

"And I'm allowed to take any measures necessary to recover him?"

Nate held her gaze, giving her one slow nod. "Yes, Ms. Satori. Bring him back by any means necessary."

"Well then, there's no time like the present. Let's get started."

# CHAPTER THREE
## FINLEY

The plush carpet ate the sound of their footsteps as they followed Nate to the medical ward. Finley knew the way, which wasn't necessarily a good thing because it allowed him to focus on the maelstrom of his thoughts rather than where they were going.

And at the core of the storm raging in his mind was the woman walking at his side.

Was Nate right?

Was Quinn his purpose?

The possibility stunned him, if only because it should not have come as such a fucking surprise. The connection should be instant. Irrefutable. A damn lightning bolt to the heart along with the sudden realization that this person was the entire reason you'd been born.

But there'd been none of those things when he'd met Quinn.

Unless he'd missed it somehow.

He'd certainly been taken by the Animagi heir, captivated in a way he could never quite explain . . . but no light bulb moments. No lightning bolts—unless you counted his attraction to her.

Yet, it made perfect sense.

It explained everything. Why he was drawn to her. Why no matter how many times he tried to tell himself to walk away, he never could. Why he had a visceral reaction to the mere thought of something happening to her. Why he'd risk his life to save hers.

Every.

Single.

Time.

And, perhaps most telling of all, why it felt like he couldn't breathe easy whenever they were apart.

Without stopping to overthink it, he linked his hand with hers, needing the connection to help reestablish some sense of order to the chaos in his head.

Quinn's graceful steps faltered, the move clearly catching her off guard, though she made no attempt to free herself. She must have picked up on his agitation because she gave his hand a tight squeeze. Her quiet reassurance brought with it a tidal wave of relief.

Finley blew out a breath he hadn't been aware of holding, feeling the tension melt out of him as he did.

She was here.

She was safe.

She was his.

He could feel Quinn's curious gaze, but he didn't allow himself to return it. If he did, he might throw her over his shoulder and portal them out of here. They didn't owe the Brotherhood anything, least of all their lives.

Okay, that wasn't strictly true.

As a sworn Brother, he owed them quite a lot. But if Nate was right, if Quinn really was his purpose, then his loyalty to her superseded all else. That meant as far as the Brotherhood was concerned, he may as well be a free agent. Any sway they'd once held over him was gone as if it never existed at all—or it would be once he made his vow.

That was simply a matter of semantics, though. Vow or no, once a Guardian discovered the one they were born to serve, that individual became the star in the center of their personal universe. The fixed point they revolved around. That's just the way it was. The way it always had been and would always be.

The Brotherhood knew better than to interfere with fate. Their entire order was built upon the principle of finding and safeguarding their one true purpose. It was the entire reason they'd been created. Why they even existed. Nothing was more important.

Technicalities regarding Finley's loyalties aside, helping them wasn't his choice to make. If Quinn wanted to save Marquez, he'd be right there, watching her back every step of the way. If she chose not to, then he'd get her out of there, no questions asked. And God help anyone foolish enough to try to stop them.

"His room is right up ahead," Nate said, forcing Finley to tuck his thoughts away as he indicated a red door halfway down the corridor.

Finley immediately frowned at the door's vibrant hue. A door that color in the medical ward had one very specific meaning.

*Danger.*

Perhaps he should have expected it. Nate hadn't downplayed the seriousness of Marquez's situation, but the flash of red still caught him completely off guard. If this had been an actual hospital, hazmat suits would be required to cross the threshold due to the virulent nature of whatever illness the patient had contracted.

But this wasn't a hospital, and they weren't dealing with viruses.

Finley ran a hand over the scruff on his jaw, not sure why the warning rattled him so deeply. The Guardian's affliction was magical in nature, and magic rarely acted with any sort of logic. That made it unpredictable, especially when dealing with something they hadn't come across before.

As far as protocol was concerned, Nate and the team caring for Marquez had done exactly what they should have. It was always better to be overcautious than under-prepared. So it was best to assume they'd be facing the worst.

Even knowing it, Finley couldn't shake off his unease as Nate slid the door open and stepped inside.

"Everything all right?" Quinn asked softly when Finley didn't make any move to follow.

He stared at the empty doorway and then glanced down at her. "Just feels a bit like someone walked over my grave."

"How auspicious."

She was mocking him, but the faint creases lining either side of her eyes spoke to her own concern.

"I'll feel better once we're home," he admitted. "Everything we've been through with Mikel in the last few weeks has me jumping at shadows."

Quinn tilted her chin up and whispered her lips over his. It was barely even a kiss, but it had what he was sure was the intended effect because the second her mouth connected with his, he was wholly focused on her.

As she pulled away, she whispered, "Me too, so let's hurry." Then she smirked and poked him in the chest, right above the pocket containing his ill-gotten gains. "It's a bit drafty in here."

He chuckled, her tease doing what logic had not. Feeling resolved, if not exactly confident, Finley and Quinn stepped inside, his palm resting at the small of her back as he guided her into the room. He was already so attuned to her he didn't miss the slight shiver that worked its way down her spine at the casual touch.

*Later, princess.*

He knew she couldn't hear him, but when her shoulders relaxed and her face slightly turned toward his, he would have sworn she felt his unspoken promise.

"Finley, Quinn, I'd like to introduce you to Tomas."

As one, they turned to face the dark-haired man standing at the far side of the room, staring blankly at the wall. He didn't even flinch.

"I thought he was unconscious," Quinn murmured, gesturing at the unmoving figure. "I was sort of expecting him to be in a bed . . . or a coma."

"He may as well be. He's certainly not cognizant," Nate said, tucking his hands into his pockets.

That was obvious enough. The Guardian certainly didn't register the sound of his name, let alone their presence in his room.

Quinn pursed her lips as she cast her gaze around. "This place is giving off more of a psych ward vibe than a medical one."

She wasn't wrong.

Everything inside was a pale, neutral gray, the same miserable color as a winter sky and just as cold. The walls were padded, the floor spongy, and the air was thick with the scent of disinfectant and despair. Add in a cot or one of those chairs with the built-in restraints, and the scene would be complete. Not that the man in the corner seemed as though he needed to be restrained. It was hard to tell if he was even breathing from here.

Finley moved deeper into the room, studying his fellow Guardian with interest. He'd heard of Tomas Marquez but had never met the man. Known throughout the agency for his tracking abilities, Tomas had a stellar reputation. It was rumored that he could find anyone. A claim he'd proven time again with the sheer number of cold cases he'd solved when no one else could.

He was also notorious for working alone. Something about how the minds and opinions of others got in his way. Sadly, that was probably the reason he'd been trapped by whatever spell did this to him. He hadn't had anyone to watch his back.

"What's that?" Quinn asked, pointing to a monitor filled with dozens of animated charts.

Nate's gaze flicked in the direction she'd indicated. "Those are his vitals."

Her eyes were round as she looked between Marquez—who still hadn't so much as blinked since they entered—and back to the screen on the wall.

"But I don't see any wires or machines."

"We injected a device into his neck. It sends the information we need to our healer's computer, which is summarized on the screen."

"That seems a little extreme."

Nate shrugged. "Given the state he's in, he could hardly tell us what happened, let alone how he was feeling."

"And you went with an implant instead of anything remotely less invasive?"

"Our plan was to sedate him so we could run tests, but every time we tried, he fought us off. Marquez may be checked out mentally, but he doesn't like being touched."

Quinn frowned at that. Her gift didn't require touch, but it was far more effective when combined with a physical connection. Finley had no doubt, given what they were up against, that she'd been counting on the boost such contact would provide. Luckily, she had him and the aid of his substantial magic to bolster hers. It should more than make up for any deficit.

"I don't understand how his body can have that level of autonomy without the aid of his mind," she said after a minute, shaking her head as if she was struggling to work out some kind of puzzle.

Nate shrugged. "I wish I could tell you, Ms. Satori—"

"Quinn," she corrected automatically.

"And I was doing so well," he said with a small smile. "Apologies, Quinn. Some habits are harder to break than others." Smile fading, he let out a resigned sigh. "It baffles us as well, to be honest. But as far as we can tell, Marquez's conscious mind is trapped while his body functions on autopilot. Sort of like a robot without the aid of its own AI. All basic functions, no finesse or complex thought."

Quinn pressed her lips together. "This is all sounding very futuristic. I thought you guys were experts of the magical arts, not science."

Finley laughed. "Back in my day, science *was* magic."

"Okay, Gramps," Quinn said, holding up both hands as if waving him off at the pass. "No need for you to blather on about how you used to ride your triceratops through the snow uphill both ways. We get it. Times have changed since the Dark Ages."

Nate let out a loud bark of laughter, then quickly turned away and tried to disguise his mirth as a coughing fit.

Finley was used to Quinn's sharp tongue, so her dig came as less of a surprise to him. Still, his lips twitched as he swallowed back his own laugh, barely managing to keep his comeback to himself.

*I prefer it when you call me Daddy.*

Since they had an audience, he made do with the much more polite, "Just how old do you think I am?"

"Ancient," she replied, her face carefully blank, though he caught the mischievous sparkle in her eyes.

"Sometimes it feels that way," he replied blandly, making her snicker.

"That it does," Nate said, once he recovered enough to turn around.

Quinn looked far too pleased with herself. Though, he supposed she had every right to since she'd just successfully staved off the oppressive atmosphere threatening to take over. It was hard not to be crushed under its weight when faced with the truth of what they were up against. She'd sensed it and acted instinctively. He'd spent enough time with her to recognize that laughter was her weapon of choice against the darkness. Her way of reminding herself, and those she cared about, that hope still existed even when it felt as if the deck was stacked against them.

She'd done it plenty of times for Lina, and now she'd done it for him.

He'd always loved that about her, and he hardly minded being the butt of her joke. Even so, he'd make her pay for her impertinence. Likely with his hand riding her pert arse.

As soon as the image bloomed to life in his mind, he knew it had been a mistake. He couldn't afford the distraction of such tempting thoughts. One hint of what he had planned for them, and his cock ached for relief. He hadn't had this much trouble focusing on a case . . . well, ever.

*Bloody hell.*

He wasn't sure who he'd been trying to prove a point to back in Nate's office. The game had started off as a way to distract her, to provide her with a little taste of what was to come. But he should have known better. One taste was never enough. Even with the threat of the case and everything that could go wrong looming over them, Finley was still suffering from the side effects of his game.

*Christ.*

If something as simple as a pair of panties could affect him so profoundly, he'd be a fucking goner once he had a chance to properly learn her body.

Finley sucked in a breath, forcing himself to stay in the present before his wayward thoughts ran wild picturing all the ways he'd do just that. He comforted himself with the knowledge that after today, he'd have an entire lifetime to map out all the places she liked to be touched and discover new ways to make her squirm. Quinn was his reward for getting over this one last hurdle. Everything he'd ever wanted was within reach; all it required was a little more patience.

He looked at her with no little heat, causing her cheeks to flush under the intensity of his gaze. She blinked at him, doing nothing to conceal her own yearning as she returned his stare.

*Ballsy little minx.*

The way she stared at him, silently daring him to give them both what they craved, had him ready to haul her out of here and to the nearest supply closet. But no. Quinn deserved far more than a hurried fuck against a wall or on top of a random desk.

Though he'd be lying if he said the idea didn't hold significant appeal. Maybe if they could just take the edge off, it would help them focus.

Finley swallowed back a growl and mentally shook his head, shoving the thought away for both their benefits.

Job first, then they'd play. For her, he'd be patient.

Even if it killed him.

# CHAPTER FOUR
## FINLEY

"So, what do you think? Are you up for it?" Nate asked, looking uncharacteristically anxious.

As long as Finley had known the man, he'd never seen him break a sweat. Not even amid battle. Nate's cool head was legendary. It's the main reason they'd handed him the temporary Director seat over men twice his age. Finley knew it was only a matter of time before they made the placement permanent. No one wanted another shit show, and Nate was one of the few who could weather the storm left in the wake of his predecessor.

Quinn sighed. "Well, this certainly changes things."

"How so?" Nate asked, radiating tension. Once again, the Guardian directed his question to Quinn, clearly recognizing she was the one in the driver's seat.

It was a refreshing change of pace for Finley. He'd led more than his fair share of these investigations and was happy to let her take charge. He almost preferred being there for moral support versus bearing all the responsibility himself. Almost.

Control was pretty nonnegotiable for him when he had a say in the matter. He'd spent too many years of his life without any to willingly cede it now. But in this instance, for her, it felt right. She was the expert here, and he had no trouble admitting her telepathic abilities greatly surpassed his own. Not to himself or anyone else who asked. She'd inherited her power while he'd been gifted with his. In his experience, natural talent almost always beat out something learned.

She crossed her arms, leveling Nate with a look. "For starters, if Tomas is still capable of moving around and walking away, it's going to make it nearly impossible to keep the connection established once we start. It would be far easier for everyone involved if he was secured."

"You mean restrained."

Quinn looked apologetic as she nodded. "I know he's your friend, and it may not be ideal, but it really is the safest way for us to help him."

"No, no, you're right." Nate blew out a heavy breath. "Honestly, the only reason we haven't done so already is that he hasn't displayed any sign of violent behavior."

"Except for the times you touched him," Finley said.

"Right. Touch is a definite trigger, but easily avoided." The skin around Nate's eyes tightened as if he just realized it might not be such a black and white matter for them. "You won't need to rely on that, will you?"

Quinn gave Marquez a wary once-over. "Not if I can help it."

Without warning, she crossed the room.

Finley sucked in a sharp breath, his adrenaline spiking as he watched her move away. Despite Nate's assurances, he still feared the Guardian's reaction to a stranger approaching him in his current state. He needn't have worried. Marquez didn't bat an eye. Not even when she circled around to stand in front of him.

She remained a respectful distance as she studied her subject, whispering something Finley didn't quite catch. He counted the seconds as they all waited for a reaction.

But there wasn't one. It was as if she wasn't even there.

Quinn didn't seem surprised by that, and she bit her lip and gave a slow nod. Then she completed the rest of her circle, her eyes scanning Marquez from head to toe as she did. Once her inspection was complete, she rejoined them.

"Well?" Nate prompted.

"We'll give it our best shot."

Realizing she'd spoken for both of them, she glanced at Finley. He read the apology in her eyes and shook his head, letting her know there was nothing to apologize for.

Finley knew he didn't imagine Nate's relief as the man's entire body relaxed. "That's all I can ask. Thank you, Quinn."

"Don't thank me yet. I haven't done anything. And I'm not sure how long this will take. It could take minutes, hours, or it could require multiple sessions over the course of several days. There's no way to know until we get in there, but I feel obligated to warn you, the longer it takes, the less likely it is we'll be successful."

Concern flickered in Nate's gaze, but his expression remained impassive. It appeared Quinn's willingness to try was all he'd needed to return to his usual cool-headed state. "Is there anything special you'll require?"

She looked around, assessing the room. "Just a safe space to work and some chairs."

"Of course. Does this suit your needs, or would you like me to find you something else?"

"Here is fine, so long as we aren't interrupted."

Nate removed his tie, his eyes glowing with power as he accessed his magic and transformed the slender length of silk into a hospital bed and two comfortable-looking chairs.

"For a second, I almost thought Lina was here," Quinn said with an admiring smile. "I'm so used to her being the one creating objects out of thin air. I forget sometimes you guys can do it as well."

"For what it's worth, it wasn't exactly thin air, but I do what I can."

"Considering *that* used to be a single tie, I'd say you can do quite a bit."

"How come he gets all the compliments?" Finley asked, unable to rein in his sudden jealousy. "Nord and I have done the same for you countless times, and you may as well yawn for all the interest you show."

"Oh, I'm sorry, Batman. Are you feeling jealous? Does your *ego* require a little stroking?"

His eyes narrowed as Nate laughed. He gave her a warning shake of his head, promising retribution with his gaze. Nate was smart enough to hide his smile. Quinn less so. Though, to be fair, that was nothing new. It was his belief she didn't have an ounce of self-preservation when it came to him.

He intended to use the knowledge to his advantage once they were alone.

The door swung open, interrupting their staring contest before it devolved into something decidedly less innocent.

One of the Brotherhood's junior healers strode inside without waiting for permission, meaning Nate had likely summoned him as soon as Quinn okayed the space.

"While he gets Tomas ready, how about we step into the adjoining room and I can forge the link between your minds?" Nate asked, sliding open a pocket door and revealing a small suite just beyond.

"Is it . . . safe to leave him without backup?" Quinn asked.

Nate looked over at the healer, his lips twitching. "Don't let his size fool you. Oliver knows how to take care of himself. He'll be just fine."

She looked dubious but eventually stepped into the suite. Looking around at the single bed, bedside table with its lone lamp, and the modest bathroom, she asked, "Is this standard?"

"Partners and family members appreciate having a place nearby. Especially when a Guardian's injury requires an extended stay," Finley explained.

A furrow appeared between her brows, and it didn't require a telepathic link to figure out what she was thinking. She wanted to know where Tomas' family was. The sad truth, however, was that most members of the Brotherhood didn't have any to speak of—besides each other.

After a few seconds, Quinn blinked and refocused on Nate. "What do we need to do?"

"You don't have to do anything. Just relax and allow me to take care of this," he said with a warm smile.

"Famous last words."

Finley understood Quinn's unease. He didn't like people fumbling around in his mind either. It might seem hypocritical, but only someone who regularly experienced the depravity and chaos in the minds of others knew to cherish the solitude of their own.

He took her hand in his, hopefully conveying without words that she had nothing to fear from him. He had no intention of straying where he wasn't welcome. Her mind and memories were her own. He much preferred when she willingly shared those parts of herself. Each new layer she revealed felt like a victory, and he didn't want to rob either of them of the experience.

Nate clearly noted the casual touch and its implied intimacy, but didn't comment on it. "All right, this is common enough for you, Fin, so just hang out while I explain the process. Quinn, have you ever lowered your mental barriers before?"

She nodded, though she looked a little nauseated.

"Then this will be familiar to you as well. Just close your eyes and when I brush against the edge of your mind, let me in. I promise not to go past the surface, and it will only take me a second to forge the mental pathway."

"So how does it work once it's in place?" Quinn asked as she closed her eyes.

"It's the same basic process I use to create portals," Finley told her. "But instead of tethering two specific places together, the connection is established between two minds."

"So you're creating a portal for thoughts to travel between our minds?"

"It's more like a bridge, but the physics of it are essentially the same," Finley said.

"I thought this was magic, not science."

"I told you they can be the same thing."

A smile ghosted across her lips, but she immediately schooled it. "Poh-tay-toe, poh-tah-toe."

"Exactly."

"You ready?" Nate asked.

Quinn inhaled deeply. "Go ahead and rip the Band-Aid off, doc."

"Just remember, once you're done with the mission, I'll be happy to sever the link if that's what you want."

Finley knew the reassurance was for her benefit, to ensure that she was comfortable moving forward, but a part of him protested it anyway. He didn't like the idea of anyone fiddling around with a connection once it was established between them.

Quinn tensed as Nate rested his hands on her shoulders. The minor act of vulnerability made Finley swell with protective need. It was completely unnecessary on both their parts. Sliding into someone's mind was as easy as dipping your toes into a smooth pool of water. It didn't hurt or feel like anything at all, really.

At least, not until the two separate consciouses merged. That part always felt unsettling. Sort of like the way hair could brush against the back of your neck, and for a second, you mistook the feeling as someone else's fingers. It was the barest ghost of a touch, just enough of a warning to send shivers racing down your back and warmth flowing across your skin.

Even though he knew it was coming, the merger still came as a surprise. Both of them gasped, and goosebumps raced down Finley's arms as his mind underwent a sudden expansion. One second he was just Finley, and the next, he'd acquired a new awareness. One that had never existed in his mind.

This was . . . unexpected. Different. He'd never felt *completed* like this before. As if Quinn had always been meant to be there, an established fixture in his mind, and he hadn't realized she'd been missing until now.

"I can feel you," she said with a shaky laugh.

They shared a look, and he wondered if she was experiencing the same rush. If his presence also felt like a piece of her she hadn't known existed had just come home.

"The connection will feel less foreign in time," Nate assured them. "But you'll be hyper-aware of it for the next few days, which actually works in your favor with the mission. It'll help keep you grounded in the present. Sort of like a sore tooth. The more you touch it, the more you feel it. But, eventually, you'll get used to the ache and learn to live with it. Or rip it out."

Quinn snickered. "That's Finley. The constant aching pain in my *tooth*."

Her overly dramatic emphasis made it abundantly clear what she really meant.

Finley laughed along with Nate, though his amusement had more to do with the fact that he now had a private way of getting back at her. One he couldn't resist exploiting right now.

His words were a seductive whisper along their newly established bond. *"Oh, come on, princess. Imagine the possibilities. Think of all the ways a connection like this could come in handy. Like when I want to tell you to come for me, but my tongue is buried in your sweet cunt."*

Quinn stumbled, which was amusing since she'd been standing completely still. She tossed him an annoyed glance, although there was no mistaking the desire sparking to life in her plum-colored irises. *"Or perhaps I'll be the one telling you to come while you fuck my throat."*

The hard-on he'd only just gotten under control surged back to attention, and Quinn smirked as he adjusted himself. He read the challenge in the slight tilt of her chin and lifting of her brows. As if she was throwing down the gauntlet and asking him what he was going to do about it.

Fuck, but he loved her fire.

*"I think you mean beg me to let you come."*

She rolled her eyes. *"Last I checked, I didn't require permission or help for that. Besides, I have two hands, one to play with your balls and one to slide between my legs."*

Finley let out a choked laugh, hating that he couldn't make use of the small bed beside them. There were a few lessons he needed to teach his impertinent princess.

Once again, it was Nate who pulled them both back to the present, this time by clearing his throat, color high on his cheeks. He shot Finley a look as he adjusted the knot of his newly restored tie. "Jesus, man, I can't hear you two, but I can certainly feel the vibes you're throwing off. I'm going to need a cold shower just from being in range of all this sexual tension."

Finley laughed. He'd accused Nord of the same thing many times.

"I'd apologize, but I'm not sorry," he said.

Quinn snickered. "You never are, Batman."

"I need some way to keep you on your toes, vixen. Otherwise you'd walk all over me. Pushing your buttons is the only way to garner any respect."

She pursed her lips, making him ache with the need to kiss her. "It's true."

Nate scrubbed a hand over his face. "Fuck the shower. I'm just going to take a walk in the snow. Naked as the day I was born. Make a snow angel or two. That should do it."

"Sounds like a good way to lose some friends," Quinn said with a pointed look at Nate's trousers.

Taking pity on his friend, Finley brought the subject back to neutral territory. "Is there anything else we need to know before we go in?"

Nate instantly sobered. "Keep your eyes open. Search for the memory of what happened, specifically any trace of the person who might have done this to him. See what clues you can find. We don't have a record of anyone with a gift like this, so it could be someone new to the scene. It could also be the start of a series of new attacks against the Brotherhood. Anything you find could be vital."

"Of course," Finley promised.

Beside him, Quinn offered her own assurance, but he could tell by the grim set of her lips that she didn't like the idea that this might not be an isolated event. They just got done dealing with one psychopath; they didn't need another one right on his heels.

The reminder of Mikel set a memory flickering to life in the back of his mind. Something Lina mentioned in passing.

Just the thought of it sent ice running through Finley's veins.

In his final moments, Mikel had warned Lina his death would only be the beginning. An event that would set countless others into motion, things they'd never predict. His death would be the catalyst of a new era, one comprising destruction and chaos.

His true legacy.

Finley hadn't given it much thought at the time. Why would he? Mikel was dead. They'd all chalked his speech up to a dying man's last-ditch attempt to foster fear. But it was a lot harder to ignore the sinister threat when faced with unfamiliar magic that had ensnared one of their own and refused to let go.

Could this be related to him in some way? Had Mikel really found a way to retain his chokehold on the realm of the living from beyond the veil? Finley was no stranger to monsters, but he shivered at the possibility.

Quinn must have caught the involuntary movement because she looked up at him sharply. *"What is it? What's wrong?"*

He shook his head, not wanting to worry her needlessly if his assumption was incorrect. Mikel had blackmailed and manipulated her enough. Knowing he was the potential culprit would only impede the job she needed to do. As for him, the knowledge would help him stay focused. Because if it *was* Mikel they were dealing with

—even indirectly—things were far, far worse than they could have imagined.

As they shuffled back into the other room to take their place at Marquez's side, Finely couldn't help but wonder, if Mikel was responsible for all of this, what the hell would be waiting for them in the Guardian's mind?

# CHAPTER FIVE
## QUINN

The first time she'd ever entered someone else's mind, it had been an accident. She hadn't even realized she'd done it until the images blooming behind her eyelids no longer belonged to her. Thankfully, Lina had been too preoccupied with the horrors of her childhood to realize Quinn had slipped in.

They'd barely been six years old when Evalina's father started summoning her to his office. All Quinn knew at the time was her happy, bubbly friend disappeared in more ways than one as soon as the door swung shut behind her. The two of them would be out playing, Lina would leave to see him, and she'd return diminished. Her joy stripped away from her like a flower plucked of all its petals.

On one such occasion, Quinn dropped her arm around Lina's shoulders, fiercely wishing there was something she could do to take the sadness from her eyes. But when she'd asked what was wrong, Lina bit down on her lip and shook her head, not only refusing to talk about it, but not speaking at all for the next three days. Of course, Quinn hadn't known it would take so long for her friend to return at the time.

The broken look in her ocean-blue eyes had been more than

enough to send the spark of Quinn's desire to help into a full-blown inferno. The next thing she knew, the memory was right there in her mind, playing out like her own personal movie. Lina sat in a chair in front of her father while he hurled insults at her, one after another, each one louder and more degrading than the last. The shock of it was enough to shove Quinn's consciousness right back out.

Parents were supposed to protect, nurture, and love their children. Never harm. Never break. But that's exactly what Anatoly Cuska had done. Day after day, year after year. His pain turned him into a cruel husk of a man who couldn't look at his daughter without seeing what she'd stolen from him: the love of his life. Instead of cherishing the child who was all he had left of his wife, when he looked at her, all he saw was a murderer.

From the day Lina had been born, he'd hated her with an icy fury that never abated. And his nearly constant verbal abuse had destroyed any illusion she might have that her own father loved and wanted her. Six was far too young an age to learn that painful truth.

Quinn had clutched Lina tighter, shaking with muted fury on her best friend's behalf. She remembered that day so vividly. Not just because it was the first time she'd used her powers, but because it was the exact moment she'd learned to hate.

Lina never knew what Quinn had seen, not even now. Her best friend's torment at the hands of her father was hers to share when and if she wished. A person had a right to their trauma. But from that day on, Quinn made it her personal mission to stay close. To never leave Lina alone with Anatoly if it could be avoided.

She even went so far as to tell her mother all girls deserved to grow up with a mom and asked Cora to adopt Lina. They never really discussed it, but Quinn knew her mom had guessed the reason she'd been so insistent about Lina coming to live with them because soon after that, the Cuska heir spent more nights at the Satori house than her own.

Quinn hadn't thought of that first time in decades, and it struck her as odd that it came back to her now. Like it was a portent she should heed, but it left her uneasy because she couldn't make sense of it.

Which was ridiculous.

After decades of experience, why should this time be any different?

It had always been easy for her to shift her consciousness into someone else's mental plane. Her power allowed her to peel back their mental layers and reveal all their secrets. Not only that, she could take control of them. She did it as easily as a summer breeze drifting across the glassy surface of a lake, sending little ripples cascading out in every direction. What she commanded, they obeyed —whether they wanted to or not.

No mind was safe from her.

Not after she Ascended.

Lina had once compared her to a pirate commandeering ships at sea. As much as Quinn loved the metaphor, she disagreed. It was true some of her takeovers were hostile, but her methods involved much more finesse. While she could make people aware of her interference, she preferred to wield her power like a scalpel, not a sledgehammer.

In every mind, there were a series of invisible threads that she could pull and pluck as needed. She supposed that's why the Animagi referred to her as a weaver. But to her, it felt more like she was holding the strings of a marionette versus a tapestry. All she had to do was pull on the right one, and her puppets would perform exactly as she wanted them to.

If people had any idea of the full extent of her power, they would run in fear. As it was, most simply assumed her gift was tied strictly to memory. Perhaps that had been true when she'd been younger. But her gift had matured along with her until she couldn't just see memories; she could provide false ones and remove or cut away what she didn't want someone to remember.

And that was before she inherited the full extent of her power.

Now, her word was law.

A whispered command from her lips could seize the air from a person's lungs until they collapsed dead at her feet. It was only her own rigid set of morals that prevented her from abusing her gift and becoming a true monster. The world could be her oyster; she just didn't want it.

That was the biggest difference between her and men like Mikel. They'd kill without question, wielding their magic as a weapon to inflict the deepest, most horrific wounds they were capable of. Just because they could.

But power held no appeal to her. She'd seen too many good people corrupted by it. And while she may ally herself with villains from time to time, she had no intention of becoming one. Really, she was a fucking saint. How many people willingly tear up a winning lottery ticket?

A simple life filled with simple pleasures. That's all she'd ever wanted. Good food. Loyal friends. Fine clothes. A sexy Brit with a fondness for dirty talk, a body made for pleasure, and a talent with his tongue and cock that would leave her boneless and sore for days after.

Okay, so maybe the last part had only recently been added to the list.

But was that too much to ask?

Apparently so, since the universe seemed determined to keep her from actually enjoying any of it.

Quinn sighed. A gift as powerful as hers came with strings. Namely, the responsibility of doing something with it. She'd chosen to use it for good instead of evil, as annoying as that was at the moment. The reminder that this was the path she'd selected for herself was enough to help her corral her errant thoughts.

Rolling back her shoulders, Quinn cleared her mind, using the sound of Finley's measured breaths to help slow her own. It wasn't long before everything fell away. The feel of the chair against her skin. The pinch of tension in between her shoulder blades. Finley's steady presence at her side. As the world around her went silent, Quinn slid out of her body and into Tomas Marquez's mind.

Nothing in her vast experience could have prepared her for what she'd found there. Not the least of which was the flickering visage of a certain sexy Brit.

"What took you so long?" Finley asked.

Quinn startled at the sound of his voice resonating in her mind. He was standing right in front of her, close enough she could reach out and brush the tips of her fingers across his stubbled jaw, but his voice sounded from *within* her.

"What's wrong?" he asked, his brows knitting together.

"I hadn't realized the bond would allow me to see you while we were in here."

He tipped his head as if considering. "I don't think that's the bond. At least I've never heard of such a thing happening before. Must be all you."

Quinn frowned, not liking the idea that her power could still surprise her. It wasn't like she'd ever walked through a mind with someone else before, so she had nothing to base the experience on. But Finley's projection *was* different, and when faced with the chaos of Tomas' mind, she wasn't a fan of her own gift acting in unexpected ways. She needed predictability to stabilize and anchor her. How else was she supposed to know if things went wrong?

Finley tucked his hands in his pockets as he glanced around, the mannerism so patently *him* Quinn couldn't help but wonder which one of them was responsible for it. If she was the one who gave him a physical form, was she also in charge of its actions? Or was he? Was he a figment of her imagination, or had she found a way to actually give shape to his unique consciousness?

Feeling a headache building in the base of her skull, Quinn let the matter go. It wasn't like the answer held any bearing on what they were doing. She needed to focus on the reason they were here.

"Have you ever seen anything like this?" Finley asked.

"No. Never."

Which was another thing that bothered her.

While each mind was unique, they were all set up in a similar way. Quinn had come to think of them like office buildings. Each one had a reception area, the place she'd find herself when she first entered. Generally, this was a sterile, boring space, filled only with surface thoughts and stimuli. But as she'd move higher into the structure, more and more secrets would be revealed. The floors themselves would vary depending on the person, yet all served the same function. Storage. They could be categorized chronologically, by the importance of a specific person in their lives, or by something else entirely. And at the very top, the penthouse as she liked to think of it, were the flagstone memories. The most pivotal moments in a person's life. The ones that made them who they were.

At least, that's how the mind was usually arranged.

But not this one.

Tomas' mind, in a word, was broken.

Instead of an empty space filled with surface-level thoughts, Quinn and Finley were standing in a room filled with thousands of moving staircases, not one of which was the same. They were all of differing heights, shapes, and designs. As if the staircase itself was the only clue as to what it would reveal.

That would be helpful . . . if they had any way of knowing how to decipher the code. Alas, Tomas was the only one with a key, and Quinn had never met the man, so she couldn't even hazard a guess as to any possible meaning his subconscious had assigned.

"Why stairs?" Finley asked.

"Broken elevator," Quinn murmured without thinking.

"Come again?"

She hesitated before answering. For her, it was obvious—when an elevator was out of service, you had to take the stairs. But perhaps Finley's experience in other people's minds differed from hers, and her analogy was too abstract. She opted for a different explanation.

"The spell he came into contact with shattered his mind. There's no longer a linear path to his core self. Everything exists in this single room."

"So the stairs represent the various memories."

"That's my guess."

"How are we supposed to find him? We can't possibly search all of these."

"Not in time," Quinn agreed.

Frankly, she had absolutely no idea where to start. And wandering around without a strategic path was out of the question. Not just because time was of the essence, but because they could easily get lost. And if they did, there was no one else coming to lead them back out.

Before a true panic spiral could start, the answer came to her.

"We need to find the touchstone."

"You mean the foundational memories?" Finley asked, his faceted eyes searching hers.

Quinn shook her head. "No, these are different. The memories you're thinking of I would consider building blocks. The ones I'm referring to are more sentimental. Think of them as the comfort object of the mind."

"Like a child's stuffed bear."

"Or a bubble bath and bottle of wine after a long day. Anything that reduces stress and provides the brain with a much-needed endorphin rush."

Finley smirked at her explanation. "Not exactly what I would choose."

She arched a brow. "Oh? I suppose you'd prefer a joy ride in one of your fancy cars?"

"Wouldn't even make the top ten."

"Really? Okay, I'll bite. Dazzle me, Batman. How do you self-soothe?"

He shrugged, his dimple flashing. "I prefer something more . . . interactive."

This might be a mental game, but Quinn had a very physical reaction. "Jesus, I walked right into that."

"Come on, princess. Don't tell me a few Os don't go a long way to improving your mood."

"Sure they do, but I'm not talking about simply relieving tension, Batman. We're not looking for the guy's mental spank bank. I'm referring to the kinds of memories you turn to in your darkest moments. The ones that make you feel safe. Remind you of the times you were truly happy."

His expression shuttered, and he looked uncharacteristically bleak. "I see. And what memory is your touchstone, Satori?"

The answer came to her lips immediately. It wasn't the sort of thing she'd usually share because of how much it revealed about her, but she was speaking before she even realized she wanted to.

"It was the night before my father was executed."

Finley's body language didn't change, but his gaze sharpened, his focus wholly on her. It was a heady feeling to know she had one hundred percent of this man's attention. That he was interested enough in learning about her to shut out everything else.

"It was the first snowfall of the year, and my mom was so excited. She loves the snow, how it blankets everything, cocooning the world in its beauty. How it turns even the biggest eyesores in the city into something pristine and perfect, if only for a little while. Mostly, though, she likes how it sparkles. Mother Nature's diamonds, she used to tell me."

Quinn let out a little laugh, her heart full and aching in equal measure.

"Anyway, I wasn't even supposed to be awake, but I heard them whispering, so I crept out of bed just in time to see my father sweep my mother into his arms like she was a grand lady and he some dashing lord. It started off as a joke, him leading her through a made-up waltz beside the window, humming a tune completely off-key as she smiled at him like he was her favorite rock star. I'll never forget the way the glow of the fire illuminated their bodies. To me, standing in the hallway in my pajamas, it was like watching a dream come to life."

Her voice grew wistful and thick with emotion.

"I know it's not particularly special in the grand scheme of things. But to me? It was the single most beautiful thing I'd ever seen. I was still so young, too young to understand much of anything, but I *knew* I was witnessing true love.

"That was the moment I realized it wasn't about the grand gestures like you see in the movies or read about in books. It's the quiet moments. The ones no one writes about because they seem so boringly normal. But the truth is, they are the most special of them all because they're private. Not for anyone else's eyes. Shared only between two people who love each other unconditionally.

"I promised myself then and there never to settle for anything less than a man who'd give me the quiet moments. A man who knew I'd never be happy with a white knight when I could have a dance partner in the snow."

Realizing she'd said far more than she ever intended, Quinn cleared her throat, looking away from Finley's warm, knowing gaze.

"Anyway, those are the kinds of memories we need. The ones that feel well-worn and often visited. Maybe if we look for staircases that show signs of age but are still well-maintained, they'll lead us to him?"

"Sounds like a good place to start," he agreed.

Finley was wise enough not to comment on her sudden about-face, but she knew he'd made note of what she'd shared. That he'd bring it back up when it best served its purpose. The bastard never let her get away with anything. It's one of the things she loved about him. He wasn't afraid to call her on her bullshit. Lina was the only other person in her life who'd ever dared to do the same.

Without another word, Finley took her hand in his. It was a peculiar feeling because they weren't actually touching with their bodies, but she could still sense the press of a hand against her palm. Felt the same electric tingle shooting up her arm.

They moved in silence for several minutes, the stairs twirling around them in every direction as they searched for one like she'd described. Her breathing had finally returned to normal when Finley drawled, "So . . . snow, huh?"

"I fucking knew you wouldn't let that go."

But despite the annoyed snarl of her words, her heart gave a little lurch in her chest and her stomach filled with the delighted flutter of a million butterflies. He'd taken her confession to heart, accepting it like it had been some kind of challenge—one he had no intention of losing.

She had a feeling in the very near future, Finley was going to get to work providing her with the thing she'd dreamed about since she was a little girl.

The kind of love no one wrote about.

The kind of love everyone wanted.

One filled not with grand gestures but a thousand small, quiet moments.

Shivers of apprehension crawled down her spine, her happy glow fading as a voice in her mind whispered.

*A love people died for.*

# CHAPTER SIX
## FINLEY

After centuries of exploring minds with his gift, Finley was rarely surprised by what he discovered. It was rarer still that he'd come across something truly unique, and Marquez's pirouetting staircases were nothing if not unique.

He didn't trust them.

Even so, it was the silence that really unnerved him. He'd never been inside a mental plane this quiet, one without a single whisper of conscious thought.

If he hadn't seen Marquez with his own eyes, Finley would have assumed the man was dead based solely on the state of his psyche. His mind was clearly in distress. Perhaps not in an obvious or traditional way, like the chaotic riot of paintballs exploding against a canvas. Or the incoherent roar of too many conversations happening at once. Either of which would signify war was underway through the hail of sensory gunfire.

There was none of that to be found in this place. Only its lack.

A void instead of a maelstrom.

The sinister nature of the hush unnerved him, settling beneath his skin and taunting him like an itch he couldn't scratch. If not for the woman at his side, he wouldn't have ventured any deeper into this strange realm, not nearly curious enough to unveil its owner's secrets. The cloying sense of *otherness* was too strong. Like the smudge of a fingerprint on a lens, this internal landscape was blurred. Distorted. In desperate need of being wiped clean.

That would usually be enough to spur Finley to action. But not today.

Although this was a rescue mission, Tomas was far from Finley's first priority. He was here for *her*. Full stop. At the first sign of genuine danger, he was pulling the plug on the whole thing and getting them both out.

"Here, this one," Quinn said, pointing to a crumbling set of stairs in front of her.

Finley was thankful she'd found a way to give them both a physical form so she could appreciate the dubious cast of his expression. "You said well-worn, not decrepit."

Laughter twitched at her lips, though her voice was patently dry as she replied, "One man's ratty sweatshirt is another's stairway to heaven."

"What does a sweatshirt have to do with anything?"

Quinn rolled her eyes. "It was a metaphor, Batman."

"A poor one, perhaps. What you said didn't even make any sense. Metaphors are supposed to demystify convoluted theories, not further obfuscate them."

She quirked a brow and crossed her arms. "For someone who seems to know all the big words, you sure have a narrow grasp of rhetoric. Maybe you're simply too limited to appreciate the subtle genius of my analogy."

Finley snorted. "You don't do subtle. And at *best* it was a mixed metaphor."

She paused, her eyes narrowing slightly as she considered his words. Eventually, she nodded. "All right, I'll give you that. I was just trying to say that what appears to one person as an item of little worth could be valuable beyond measure to another."

He glanced back at the item in question, not bothering to conceal his grimace. "This staircase should be condemned."

"I'll be sure to let the mayor of Crazy Town know when I see him during his nightly walkabout. Think he'll bust out his monocle and top hat tonight in addition to his walking cane when he pops by to give us the ole 'Good evenin' guvna'?"

Finley quaked with laughter at her terrible cockney accent. "Please never do that again."

She tossed him a cheeky grin as she continued to bastardize the English language. "Why's that, luv? Too sexy for ya? Does it make ya want to whip out Ol' Blind Bob an' bend me over the rails so you can introduce 'im to me happy valley?"

Finley pressed the heels of his hands to his eyes, laughing too hard to format a response. When he finally recovered, he noted the wood of the banister on either side of them was pockmarked and the rails rusted through. He looked up at her with a slight shake of his head. "That dodgy thing would give way at the first sign of pressure. We'd have better luck fucking on the stairs themselves."

Quinn ran her eyes up the dingy staircase. "I'm not really a fan of rug burn, Batman. But for you, I'd at least consider it."

Finley followed her gaze, his amusement giving way to revulsion as he took in the threadbare carpet lining the steps. It was coated in all manner of stains, and as a whole, looked like something out of a horror movie, not at all like the gateway to a beloved memory. And definitely not the kind of place he'd choose to take a break to shag his woman properly for the first time.

"These are worse than the ones in Mataius' building."

Quinn jerked at the unexpected reference. "How do you mean?"

"You were so put off by their appearance you didn't even want to go near them for fear of being murdered."

A bark of laughter escaped the delicate column of her throat. "These are hardly murder stairs," she said with a shake of her head, sending all that dark raven-colored hair flying as she started up the first step. Finley watched the gentle sway of her hips as she climbed up two more before pausing and looking back over her shoulder. "Though I have to admit, I'm impressed by your recall. It's nice to know you really do pay attention when I speak."

"Was there ever any doubt?"

She lifted one shoulder in a teasing shrug. "Maybe."

He watched her take a few more steps before calling after her. "Are you sure it's this one?"

She gestured vaguely to her left. "Have we come across anything else so far that seemed like a better contender to you?"

Finley frowned as he looked back the way they'd come. There was a rope ladder, a fireman's pole, a fire escape, even a spiraling staircase with no discernible end. The only thing any of them had in common was their pristine condition. After well over a hundred variations, this truly was the first set of stairs they'd come across that had shown any sign of wear.

He sighed, swallowing back his reservations. She was the expert here, and he'd already agreed to follow her lead. If she wanted to test her theory out on a staircase that would have given Jack the Ripper pause, well . . . he couldn't exactly let her do it alone, could he?

"Lead the way," he sighed, climbing up after her.

"In case you missed it, that's what I'm already doing."

As he lifted his head to reply, the words died on his tongue. The peach shape of her arse was positioned above him, directly in his line of sight. He had the overwhelming urge to lean forward and take a bite out of it.

Quinn's laughter floated down behind her, cutting off his wandering thoughts before they strayed too far. "See something you like?"

He lifted his gaze, nowhere near repentant for being caught staring at her delectable curves. "Maybe."

Her smile stretched at his deliberate use of her own taunt. "Touché, Batman. Touché. Now stop flirting. We're almost at the top."

He was tempted to tell her to stop looking so fucking edible but managed to resist.

"After you, love."

Finley just caught the tinge of color on her cheeks and bit back a smile. She liked to play at remaining unaffected, but he was learning her tells and how to breach her defenses. For instance, barbed banter got her hot, but casual affection was the way to actually thaw her icy exterior. And a growled command? When delivered correctly, it didn't just make her melt; it shattered her resistance entirely. He couldn't wait to take advantage of the fact once they were well and truly alone.

Quinn Satori, the ball-busting, aloof Ice Queen, had already drawn him irrevocably into her orbit. But he wanted more. He wanted to discover all the messy, broken parts of her.

He knew the experience would be life-altering, which was why it was his mission to set her free. Free from the chains she locked her heart up in out of misguided fear. To not only tear down her walls but permanently obliterate them so nothing—not even her own insecurities—could ever come between them again. Because now that he'd had a taste, he'd settle for nothing less than everything.

Now that she was finally within reach, his need had become all-consuming. The tease of her drove him mad to the point that the entire day had become a study in edge play. If they didn't finish up here soon so he could take her home and sink into her sweet heat, he was going to go the way of Marquez and lose his bloody mind.

Quinn must have felt the same relentless need buzzing through her veins because they hurried the rest of the way up the staircase without another word. Neither of them stopped until the surrounding air grew thick with fog and the room they'd walked through vanished as if it had never existed. That included the stair-case, leaving them stranded in a laboratory that was, quite simply, troubling.

They hadn't entered a memory as he'd expected. At least, not in the way Finley had ever experienced. It felt more like walking onto a movie set after hours. The stage was ready, but everything that gave it life was notably absent.

Quinn frowned as she flicked her gaze around the various metal tables and the scientific paraphernalia scattered across their surfaces.

"What the hell is this?" she muttered.

"Frankenstein's lab?"

"Funny."

Finley pointed up to the skylight and the stormy clouds beyond. "All we're missing is the doctor in a lab coat and a corpse made of stitched-up parts."

Quinn chewed on her bottom lip, a flicker of concern in her gaze. "Let's hope we don't stumble across either of those." Her eyes narrowed on his face. "Why are you looking at me like that? Are you laughing at me?"

Finley schooled his expression, fighting hard to contain his grin. "I would never. I just didn't take you for someone afraid of—"

"Zombies?"

"The classics."

"Say what you will, Frankenstein's monster is the OG of zombies."

"I'm sure Mary Shelley would be delighted to hear you think so."

"You say that like you knew her."

"I've lived a long time; I've crossed paths with lots of people."

"Biblically?" Something like jealousy stormed across Quinn's face when she spoke, but it might have only been wishful thinking on his part.

He cocked his head to the side. "Would that be a problem for you?"

"Not if I'm the one benefiting from your experience, Batman." She dropped her voice, moving until there was barely an inch between them. "But I don't play nice with others. Not when it comes to you."

He'd had women make possessive claims about him before, but

none that ever sent a ripple of purely masculine pleasure coursing through his body. "Good. I don't intend to share you either."

"Good." Her red-painted lips tipped up. "Glad we understand each other." She turned away to inspect the nearest table, but he caught her wrist in his hand, holding her in place. Her brow lifted as she twisted back around. "Was there something else you wanted to say on the matter?"

"Only that you should know I'll kill any man who dares to touch what's mine."

Her eyes went molten, and her smile stretched. She rested her free hand against his chest, just above the steady thump of his heart. "Some things can't be stolen without permission."

"Such as?" he drawled, captivated by the seductive curl of her mouth.

"Me."

All the blood in his body rushed south as she leaned in, holding his gaze as she continued.

"Make me yours, Batman. Keep me blissed out in that gigantic bed waiting for us back in your penthouse, and you'll never have to worry about me wandering astray."

His voice was an octave lower than usual when he whispered back, "It's not you I'm worried about. I have no intention of allowing you to want for anything. Let alone another lover."

Her expression turned feral, her nails lightly pricking him through his shirt as she scraped down his chest and over his abdomen. His muscles leapt and twitched, eager for her attention, but he held himself still, curious to see where she was going with this.

"Then perhaps it would make you feel better if I remind you you're not the only killer in this relationship. Anyone tries to come between us, Fin, I'll deal with them myself. We've fought too damn hard—hell, we've come back from the brink of fucking death itself— just for the chance to see what it could be like between us. I'm not giving you up that easily."

He couldn't fight his grin this time as savage pride unfurled in his chest. "I'm starting to understand why Nord and Lina are so turned on by violence."

"That so?"

"Mmm," he agreed, lifting his hand so he could ghost his thumb over her plump bottom lip. As he ducked his head to replace his finger with his mouth, something rippled in his periphery, stopping him short.

His head snapped up, eyes narrowed as the hair down the back of his neck stood on end.

"Fin?" Quinn murmured dreamily, her eyes half-closed as she waited for his kiss. "Do I need to draw you a map, 'cause I've got to tell you that's not boding well—"

He wrapped his hand over her mouth, suppressing the rest of whatever else she was going to say.

He stared hard at the acid-green light flickering across a table in the corner, waiting for another flash of whatever had displaced the air, but there was nothing.

Finley wasn't relieved by the stillness. Senses could be tricked. There was only one way to know if something was hiding in plain sight.

Calling on his power, the world around him burst into thousands of glimmering gold threads as he peered into the very fabric of life itself.

*There.*

It took him less than a second to see what was wrong.

The strands that comprised Tomas' mind were tainted. A sickly green muted their golden shine. As he focused in on the place where he'd noted the disruption, a tendril slithered free, snaking toward them.

It moved faster than he'd anticipated. Faster than any living creature should be able to.

That's when he realized it wasn't a creature at all. It was pure magic. Left behind from whatever spell had ensnared the Guardian's consciousness.

And it was coming straight for them.

There wasn't time for him to think. He could only act on pure instinct as he shoved Quinn as hard and as far away from him as he could. Her scream of shock was drowned out by the roar of blood in his ears as the tendril of power shot straight through him, taking him hostage and sending him tumbling into a sea of nightmares.

# CHAPTER SEVEN
## QUINN

Quinn's first thought as she was flung from Tomas' mind did not stem from panic or concern, or any other acceptable emotion, for that matter. It was born of white-hot fury.

"That mother*fucker*."

He'd done it to her again. Sacrificed his life to save hers.

*More like abandoned me out of some misguided and outdated belief in chivalry.*

She huffed, limbs trembling under the assault of adrenaline and anger coursing through her.

As soon as his eyes glowed silver and horror twisted his face, she'd known what was about to happen. She may not have been able to see whatever his power had revealed, but she could translate his terror easily enough. She'd been in danger, and instead of trusting her to get them both out, that asshole jumped straight in front of the fucking train.

Tears clogged her throat, making it nearly impossible to suck in the air she so desperately needed. Didn't he know she was still suffering the effects from the last time he'd nearly died? That whenever she closed her eyes, the sight of him on the ground, impaled and bleeding out, haunted her? When would that tea-slurping idiot realize losing him was one of the only things she couldn't come back from? That it was her heart, not her body, that needed protecting?

And why . . . for the love of God, *why* was he so goddamn insistent on dying for her all the time? What was that supposed to prove other than how eager he seemed to be to escape her? How was she supposed to let someone in, something she'd never even contemplated before, when he was so fucking hellbent on leaving her every chance he got?

Yes. She was aware she was in the minority and that most women would swoon at the thought of the man risking it all to save them.

Fuck. That.

Dying was easy. All it required was a split-second choice, and it was over. Done.

What was impressive about that?

Nothing.

Sticking around and building a life with someone, that was the real test—the proof of true and enduring love. It was a decision that required daily commitment. An entire lifetime of choices, of choosing to be with her. To *be* hers.

That kind of choice took courage, and frankly, it was the kind of courage she was really starting to doubt Finley had. Because if he felt a fraction of what she did for him, surely he *knew* what it did to her every time he threw away his life.

And if he didn't? Well, she wasn't sure which was worse. Him knowing and still doing it, or him being absolutely oblivious to just how much he meant to her after everything they'd been through.

Either way, he kept sacrificing himself. Leaving her behind to suffer after these fucking *selfless* acts of his.

"Fuck you, Finley," she whispered, hastily wiping the tears off her cheeks. "Fuck you for leaving me again. For once, I wish you'd stop being so bloody noble and just be selfish."

As her tirade built, Quinn was aware that perhaps she wasn't entirely rational. That her emotions were getting the better of her. The truth was, she was out of her element here, but she didn't have a single fuck left to give.

The only thing she wanted right now was him.

If Lina had been around, she would have pointed out that Quinn's tears stemmed from grief, not anger, and that they pointed to the presence of deeper issues like abandonment or maybe even PTSD. She would have also mentioned that Quinn needed to confront them head-on unless she wanted to self-sabotage her best chance at happiness.

But she wasn't, so Quinn had every intention of nursing her grudge and ignoring the stable and emotionally intelligent voice in the back of her head.

Anger was what she needed right now. It was the only emotion that would help her focus on her task instead of the tortured cast of Finley's face when he'd tumbled to his knees as she'd been ripped away from him. Because if she thought about *that,* all she'd be good for was curling up in a ball and sobbing her eyes out. And this was far from the time for her to have a pity party.

Finley needed her.

Quinn curled her hands into fists, her gaze blurred as she finally looked over at his unnaturally still body seated beside her. Even though she knew what to expect, his vacant stare sent chills skittering down her spine. Never had she seen his beautiful silver-flecked eyes so devoid of emotion. So . . . empty.

Just like with Marquez, the lights were on, but nobody was home. He was locked in the chaos of his shattered mind, and if there was any hope of breaking him out, she was going to have to jump in after him.

So she honed the edge of her fury until it became her weapon. One she'd use to cut Finley free of his bindings, because once she set foot inside his mind, it would be a race against the clock. A war of wills between her and the magic holding him hostage.

The fucking battle of both their lives.

No pressure.

They might have been too late to save Marquez, but Quinn had absolutely no intention of letting the spell claim Finley. He belonged to her, and she was nowhere near finished with him yet. If it wanted her man, it would have to pry him from her cold, dead hands because that was the only way she'd ever let him go.

Which was exactly what she intended to tell the goddamn love of her life—that fucking wanker—once she was finished rescuing him. If he thought he could take a magical bullet for her and she'd be grateful for it, he was in for a rude fucking awakening.

She required far more than that.

She required a whole damn lifetime.

So Quinn was going to dive straight into the deep end, and she wasn't coming up for air unless he was safely in her arms. Because there was no way in hell she was going to let Finley take the easy way out. She worked far too hard for their happily ever after to allow him to fuck it up before it started.

Quinn sucked in a shuddering breath as her resolve filled her. She didn't know where Nate was, or if the temporary Director would be back soon and realize they'd lost Marquez—likely when the magic keeping him alive leapt out of his mind and into Finley's. But she couldn't exactly sit around to find out. They'd have to deal with the hows and whys of what happened later. Right now, the only thing that mattered was getting Finley back.

Focusing on her breathing, Quinn fought to quiet the tumble of thoughts racing through her head. Just as she was about to take the leap into Finley's mind, her phone rang.

She froze at the familiar bars of her mother's ring tone. Had it been anyone else, she would have ignored it, but if Cora was calling now, in this exact moment, it was important.

"Mama?"

Her mother wasted no time getting straight to the point. "You need to help him recognize truth from lie."

Quinn didn't ask how her mother could possibly know what was going on. She'd learned long ago that one simply accepted Cora's gift as fact and went from there.

"How do I do that?"

"Anchor him in the truth."

"Whose truth? His? It's his mind, Mama. I don't know his history well enough to spot the lies. And with the state he's in, it's not like I can trust what I find there."

"So use yours."

"My what?"

Her mother sighed as if it was obvious. "*Your* history, mon couer. You are the weaver. Present him with the memories the two of you have created together. Not the superficial ones, the pivotal moments. Those that have become the fabric of who you are together. Use your gift to teach him how to spot the difference between what is real and what is deception."

Her mother's words filled Quinn's blood with ice. She and Finley had a handful of such moments between them at best. And half of those he didn't—couldn't—remember.

Because of her.

"But I—"

"You know your man's heart, Quinn. He gave it to you long ago. Now it's up to you to help him remember why."

Quinn swallowed back a wave of nausea. She'd already known it wasn't going to be easy freeing Finley, but she hadn't imagined just *how* difficult it was going to be. How much she'd have to reveal to save him.

There was no knowing how he'd react once he'd found out what she'd done. What she'd taken. It didn't matter that he'd already guessed at it or that her intentions had been honorable. Honestly, she'd only been trying to protect him. She hadn't thought it would hurt anything since she'd never intended to cross paths with him again.

Maybe if she'd realized what fate had in store for them, she'd have handled things differently. Maybe then she wouldn't have given in. But there was no changing the past, so here they were. The damage was well and truly done. The only thing left for her to do now was strap on her lady balls and own up to it.

Why did the mere thought fill her with dread?

She'd never had a problem owning her mistakes—rare as they were. Though, to be fair, the stakes had never been this high.

If their roles were reversed, and Finley came to her with such an admission, Quinn wasn't sure she'd ever be able to trust him again. How could she? How could anyone trust a memory weaver who'd played around in their mind?

Worse, if that's how *she* felt about it, being the weaver in question, how could Quinn ever expect Finley to not only trust her, but to forgive her?

It was the exact reason she'd planned on taking her—their—secrets to the grave once he'd become a steady fixture in her life. She didn't want to risk losing him. But now her mother was telling her that giving Finley back his memories—the ones she'd so carefully removed—might be the only way to save his life.

*Fuck.*

"Mon couer?" Cora's voice burst through Quinn's anxious thoughts, acting like a momentary buoy before sending her plunging straight back into despair.

"Yes, Mama?"

"If you want a future with him, hold nothing back. I have a feeling you won't get a second chance."

# CHAPTER EIGHT
## FINLEY

The hunger reached him first. It clawed through the darkness, animating the ghosts of his past and giving voice to the echoes of his long-forgotten misery. That gnawing, never-ending ache had once been his faithful shadow, always with him, never straying far—no matter how hard he tried to run. Finley had hoped never to meet it again, but it seemed he was destined to be empty.

Forgotten.

In pain.

After the hunger came the loneliness. And then other emotions, just as vivid, just as all-consuming, right on its heels. A child's grief. A young boy's rage. A grown man's shame.

Grief at the loss of a mother's gentle kiss.

Rage at being so easily thrown away.

Shame for the deeds committed in the name of survival.

The feelings grounded him, no longer figments of his past, but tangible entities. Memories. *These* were the shades he used to paint the world into being around him.

Soon the darkness gave way to an empty London street. A place as familiar to him as the back of his hand. There were no specific landmarks, but it didn't matter. To him, they were practically interchangeable. They'd all been his home at some point.

The air was cold and so thick with smoke it was a task just to draw in breath. Realizing he could breathe, that he had form, Finley tipped his head back, expecting to feel the tickle of snow against his face, but the churning clouds above denied him.

He should have known better than to want for anything. Simple pleasures were always denied to those like him. The castoffs. The vagrants.

In a way, he was thankful for the reminder. These streets had always been his best tutor. It was there he'd learned that when a human set limits based on morals, and not basic human needs, those morals would fail. He'd been raised never to steal, never to lie, to look down on those beneath him, to see trash instead of a human soul.

And then he'd become that trash.

All that kept him from dying in a ditch or from selling his body to pay for a warm meal were the ones who took him in. The unwanted. The nameless. The forgotten. They were the ones that taught him how to survive. How to throw away the trappings of a privileged life that no longer served him and create a new set of morals defined by need, not ideals.

Steal to stay alive. Harm to protect yourself. Loyalty is never unconditional. Hunger is the only God who matters.

These were the lessons written on his soul. The ones no amount of time could ever erase.

After his grandfather died, his options were limited. Without his mother to vouch for his parentage, the new Duke of Lennox had no need for his bastard son. He already had his heir and his spare. The only purpose Finley seemed to serve was reminding the Duke of his whore wife. Which meant he served no purpose at all.

They'd come for him in the night, tossing a hood over his head, wrapping him in bindings, and stealing him away. At first, he thought someone would save him, but then he heard that cold, mocking voice telling his captors to drown him like the stray he was. That's when he'd realized it wasn't a real kidnapping. The Duke had paid these men to make it look like one so he could save face if anyone ever dared question where his youngest son had gone.

Finley was under no illusion as to the reason his kidnappers ignored the Duke's order. With his pretty eyes, soft curls, and dimples, they'd have made a killing selling him off to the highest bidder. There were always those on the lookout for such things . . . if one only knew where to look.

Only his clever mind and penchant for mischief kept Finley from becoming lost to such a fate. After a year spent sneaking around his house to avoid the Duke's wrath, he'd had no trouble with the shabby locks of his makeshift prison.

He ran, never looking back, knowing the life he'd been accustomed to was long gone. Truth be told, he'd known it was over the day his grandfather drew his last breath. He'd been the only one who didn't seem to care about the rumors regarding Finley's birth.

As he paced the empty streets with only hunger and his memories for companions, Finley came to a stop outside a familiar wooden door. He'd found himself here once before.

On that occasion, a man with metallic flecks ringing his pupils had stopped him before he could cross the street and say the words that would have irrevocably altered the course of his life. He hadn't recognized the man he'd later know as St. Aubyn, but there was something about him that urged Finley to stay and listen to his proposal instead of fleeing.

He'd spoken of the Brotherhood and offered Finley a life filled with adventure and purpose if he'd join them. Finley hadn't been particularly interested in either, but the promise of a roof over his head and three steady meals a day were more than enough to sway him. At that point, a solitary apple would have sealed the deal.

Everybody had a price. He was beyond lucky that St. Aubyn had taken a look at him and seen far more value than Finley had ever attributed to himself. He'd have sold his soul—and his body—for a hunk of day-old bread. Instead, St. Aubyn offered him not only a life-line but a whole new life.

Finley glanced to his left and right, hoping to catch sight of the dark-haired Guardian with his kind green eyes. Thinking perhaps he'd show up again just when Finley needed him the most. But St. Aubyn was nowhere to be found.

He was on his own.

With a sinking feeling curling in his gut, Finley realized that this time, he'd have to try his luck with whatever fate awaited him beyond the door. He started forward with his heart in his throat and the taste of tears and blood on his lips. With each step, the pieces of who he'd become—of who he was—fell away until he was just a young, hopeless teenage boy once more.

When only a few feet remained between him and the door, Finley slipped and tumbled forward, crashing to his knees. The snow that had been previously denied started falling thick and fast. The cold burrowed deep, making his teeth chatter. He couldn't seem to push himself back to his feet. Instead, he curled in on himself, arms hugging his cramped and aching stomach. Another time or place, it might have appeared as though he was praying.

The door creaked open, and Finley forced himself to lift his head to meet the eyes of the woman who held his destiny in her gnarled hands.

Before he could fully unfold himself, a voice reached his ears. The sultry tone seemed to simultaneously curl around him like a caress and shred him to ribbons.

"Finley, you jackass, what the hell do you think you're doing?"

His head snapped up.

The angel hovering over him looked nothing like the scarlet-haired woman he'd been expecting. Her porcelain skin was smooth, not pockmarked. Her long raven-colored hair and pearly-white teeth were real. Her clothing . . . wrong. All wrong.

Finley frowned.

She mirrored his expression. "Why are you looking at me like you've seen a ghost?"

He lifted a trembling hand toward her as he awkwardly got to his feet. "Are you my Virgil? Here to lead me out of the depths of hell to the gates of paradise? To my Beatrice?" Finley's frown deepened, the name tasting like ash on his tongue. "No . . . you wear my angel's face, but that is not her name."

She knocked his hand away. "Of course that's not my name. Get your shit together, Batman."

Unfazed, he let his hands hover just above her velvety skin, not quite touching her as his fingertips moved parallel to the perfect symmetry of her cheekbones. "Beautiful."

The angel scowled, her wine-colored eyes glittering like gemstones as her lips twisted into a grimace. "I can't believe you're falling for this crap. It's amateur-level spell work at best. You should be ashamed. I expected more from you, Finley. Snap out of it." She glanced around the snowy rubbish-strewn alleyway with distaste. "You're certainly better than *this*. Come on. Let's get you out of here."

"Who are you?" Even he heard the notes of awe and wonder in his voice.

She let out a harsh, bitter laugh. "You know, I'd be insulted by that if you weren't so clearly out of your damn mind. Or, I guess in your case, *in* your damn mind. What is this supposed to be anyway? A labyrinth constructed out of Shakespeare's London? Jesus fuck, Fin, even your madness is boring and literal."

Her words were a confusing swirl, none of them making a lick of sense. But there was something about the sound of them that sent a flood of yearning rolling through him. "Please," he whispered, eyes trained on her lips. "Your name."

A new emotion flashed deep in the backs of those aubergine irises. Something he recognized only because he was feeling it too.

Pain.

Seeing her *hurt* him. More than the hunger. More than the memories.

What he didn't understand was why.

She blew out a breath, looking away. "So much for that epic speech about my being yours if you can't even remember who I am."

"Tell me," he begged, desperate to know who this divine creature was. Why she was here. Why she made him feel this cut up inside.

When her eyes met his again, there was no missing the shimmer of tears. "It's *me*, Batman. Quinn." She swallowed, her voice little more than a hoarse whisper. "Your princess."

The sound of the endearment punched him straight through the heart. For a second, he couldn't breathe, and the only sound in his ears was the distant roar of raging wind. The world shifted and tilted, fraying at the edges.

But then the rush of sound stopped, and everything snapped back into place.

Finley blinked at her, reading the expectation in her gaze. It was obvious she wanted him to remember something, and he wished he could. If only to wipe that look from her eyes. The longer he went without responding, the more tortured it became. He may not know who she was, but there was no denying the havoc she was playing on his equilibrium.

"Fin?"

His brows lowered, the ragged cast of her voice calling to him and dredging up the nameless need to protect. His pain was manageable. Hers? Soul-crushing.

He couldn't bear it.

"Quinn," he repeated, testing the name out, savoring the feel of it in his mouth. "Are you here to save me?"

Her eyes searched his, one perfect tear hanging from her lashes before falling free and splashing down her cheek. She held out a hand, fingers visibly trembling.

"Yes."

# CHAPTER NINE
## QUINN

Brow furrows. Broody, inquisitive, insufferable brow furrows. Never had she hated the sight of a single wrinkle this much. From the second Finley locked eyes on her, that devil of a line had taken up permanent residence on his face. Broadcasting, in glaring fashion, his complete and utter lack of recognition.

Quinn had mentally braced herself for any number of fucked-up scenarios before crossing into his mental plane, but not even once had she stopped to consider the possibility his fractured mind wouldn't remember some version of her. She'd taken his feelings for her for granted. Assuming, so naively, they'd be strong enough to withstand the power of some unknown monster's spell.

There had been a second when she'd given him her name—specifically his name for her—when something seemed to click. But before Quinn could press her advantage, it had vanished. Fleeing before she even had a chance to give chase.

Her hard-fought bravado fled in the face of that lone truth, sending the full weight of the grief she'd just barely managed to keep at bay crashing down. The ember of hope she'd so stubbornly clung to didn't stand a chance against the tsunami heading straight for it.

And then, in that moment of total despair, he touched her.

Quinn's breath stuttered at the innocent contact, the soft scrape of his palm over hers sending her emotional storm scattering and her hope roaring back to life.

It only took a glance to confirm that Finley was just as affected by the gentle play of their skin. He inhaled sharply, pupils flaring wildly as he stared at her in speechless wonder.

It didn't make any logical sense. Their bodies were far from real in this realm. His was made of some part of his subconscious, hers willed into existence via her magic. Even so, there was no denying the reaction they were having to each other. Like somehow the particles and stardust used to give them form on this plane contained the same magnetic attraction to one another they'd experienced on the outside.

As if, on the most fundamental, cosmic level, their very essences not only recognized but gravitated toward one another.

Quinn's chest caved in on itself as her lungs emptied on a sigh of pure relief.

It wasn't too late. It wasn't over. *This* was her opening.

Latching onto her power, Quinn focused on the moment she wanted to recreate. The first memory in her arsenal she'd selected to help Finley regain control of himself. She spent time weaving the details, knowing the more real she could make it feel, the more likely she'd be to tear him out of the magic currently ensnaring his mind.

And if she could do that, then he should be able to start recognizing the spell's trickery and seeing through it on his own.

*Should* being the operative word.

There were a lot of unknowns at play here. She was running on her mother's advice and pure instinct. Hopefully, they'd be enough.

Satisfied with her work, Quinn willed the memory outward so it could implant itself in Finley's mind. But as soon as she dropped her hold, it fizzled out in much the same way a drop of water turns to steam when it hits a hot surface.

Growling low in her throat, she tried a different tactic, this time stitching the memory to a one-word command.

"*Remember.*"

When all Finley did was offer her a quizzical lift of his brow, it was clear that her compulsion also failed.

"Motherfucker," she grumbled, her frustration making the word harsh and clipped.

"What's wrong?"

Quinn blew out a breath, using her free hand to scrape the hair off her forehead. "The spell's hold is too strong here. It's obliterating my weaves before they can take root. This must be its epicenter," she added, though this was mostly for her benefit as she mentally searched for a way to break through the spell's defensive barriers.

It stood to reason that if the magic was strongest here, it would weaken the farther out they got. Time to test the theory.

"Come on, Batman, we're going on a field trip."

He frowned in confusion, as if she was speaking in another language and he was desperately trying to translate it. "Field trip?"

"Yeah. You know, a mini-adventure that allows us to explore new and exciting places?" When he still didn't seem to know what she was talking about, Quinn sighed. "In order to save you, I need to get you farther away from here so I can do my thing without interference."

That, at least, seemed to register because he gave her a lopsided grin that was so achingly familiar it sent her heart galloping.

"I'll happily follow you anywhere, angel."

"I'm not your angel," she bit off. "I've only just gotten used to you calling me princess—which, frankly, is a bit beneath me, don't you think? If anything, I'm a fucking queen, maybe even an empress. But I'll put up with princess because I like the way you look at me when you say it." She peeked over at him, wondering if he'd react to her use of the endearment again.

All he did was blink. But his response, when it finally came, was unexpectedly impassioned and completely disarming. "Princesses are meant to be adored. Pampered. Cherished. Queens, while magnificent, don't truly need anyone."

Quinn's heart gave a pathetic squeeze. She'd never much cared one way or the other about his growled choice of a pet name, but now that she had some insight into why he'd selected it for her, she never wanted him to call her anything else. And it wasn't just because of what it revealed about his thoughts of her, but more what it revealed about the way he thought about himself.

Finley wanted to feel needed.

Someone—or likely many someones—had made him believe he served no meaningful purpose. That he was disposable. Irrelevant. So having a person in his life who relied on him, willingly placing their happiness in his hands, was the ultimate validation. His ultimate fantasy.

As a woman who never had any intention of relying on anyone— for *anything,* let alone her happiness—the realization that she longed to be the one to give Finley his heart's deepest desire was staggering.

"I'd still rather be a princess than an angel," she muttered.

For a second, she thought she saw a hint of familiar laughter playing about his lips, but it was gone just as quickly as she noticed it.

Uncomfortably aware that her turbulent feelings were distracting her, she refocused on her mission. Finley's hand still clasped in hers, she picked a direction and stomped off down the muddy street, towing him behind her. She hadn't been lying when she called this place a labyrinth. One after the next, each new street resembled the last. No special detail differentiated the various blocks, save the corner where she'd first found him kneeling. That place must have held special significance, but the rest of this mess? It existed only to keep him lost.

"No," she groaned when she dragged him down their fourth street only to arrive at a dead end. For a fraction of a second, she thought they'd gone in a circle, but she'd been switching up her directions, so it was a mathematical impossibility.

"Is there a reason you're in such a hurry?" he asked.

"Is there a reason you're not?" she snapped. "Maybe you haven't realized it yet, but this place is the magic equivalent of quicksand. If we don't find a way to pull ourselves out, we're going to die here."

He shrugged, shockingly nonplussed. "I spent a lifetime trying to escape these streets. It wasn't until a man with a carriage arrived that I finally succeeded."

That brought her up short. "What'd he do, offer you candy?"

"What?"

Quinn pinched the bridge of her nose. "Remind me to give you the stranger danger speech later."

He may not have been familiar with the expression, but he certainly understood the sentiment because he was quick to point out, "You're a stranger."

"No, Batman, I'm fucking not." She gritted the words out through clenched teeth, certain that wherever she was, God was laughing at her. Changing the subject, she asked, "You've been stuck on these streets before?"

Finley gave her a slow nod.

"These specific streets?"

He glanced around. "One's as good as another. They're all essentially the same."

Well, that was one mystery solved. He'd just unknowingly answered her unspoken question about why the blocks appeared nearly identical. As far as his subconscious was concerned, they were.

On the heels of that knowledge bomb came another.

"Finley . . . did you *live* on these streets?"

"I'm not sure that's the word I'd choose. More like survived."

A sudden wave of nausea made her stomach dive and swoop. "But I thought you were the spoiled son of some fancy aristocrat."

There was an unmistakable edge to his voice as he replied, "I was . . . on paper. But the matter of my true parentage was a bit of a sticking point with the Duke of Lennox, so he got rid of me."

Such stories were commonplace, especially in that day and age. It was a lot easier to make people disappear before the dawn of the internet. But she was still stunned by his admission. She'd had no idea as to his true upbringing. He'd buried it more deeply than she'd done with Lina's corpse.

"Wait. Wasn't the Duke of Lennox a Scot?"

For some reason, that made Finley grin. "You know your peerage."

She tapped a finger to her temple. "This thing's a steel trap. No fact left behind and all that."

He chuckled, and the warmth of it had goosebumps running along her arms. "That seems convenient."

"More like painful. And loud."

Instead of debating the point, he conceded. "Yes, I imagine it would be. There are many memories I wish I could forget. I can't imagine being plagued by all of them indefinitely."

Well, shit. Mr. Perpetual Stick Up His Ass was the first person who ever got it. Everyone else always treated her eidetic memory like some kind of rare gift. And maybe it was . . . just not to her.

They'd turned down another street at random when Quinn glanced at him from the corner of her eye.

"I can feel you looking at me."

"I'm just wondering about something . . ."

One side of his mouth curled up. "You want to know about my accent."

"How'd you guess?"

"You're not the first."

"Did you ditch it on purpose?" she pressed when he didn't provide any additional information.

"It hardly seemed prudent to hold on to it when the people I was begging from saw it as just another mark against me. The English were hardly inclined to help their own, let alone a Scottish cur."

Quinn frowned, chewing on the inside of her cheek. "Didn't it bother you, being forced to give up that part of your heritage?"

Finley shrugged. "I was more interested in how I was going to get my next meal. There wasn't much I wasn't willing to do to get it. Switching up how I pronounced my words was hardly the worst thing I had to do. Besides, these streets are as much a part of me as Scotland ever was. Just because you're born somewhere doesn't make it your home."

"I suppose that's true," she said, her voice heavy. Her heart ached for the little boy he'd been and the choices he'd been forced to make.

Picking up on her sadness, he nudged her with his shoulder. She glanced up at him, realizing with a little jolt that there was a clarity in his eyes that had been missing until now. A knowing spark that almost always preluded a flirtatious or teasing remark.

"Why so disappointed, lass?" he asked, his lilting Scottish brogue surprising enough to stop her dead in her tracks. "Do 'ya have a preference for men from the highlands?"

If she did, she hadn't realized it until right that moment. Suddenly the only thing she wanted was for them both to live long enough for her to find out what it sounded like when he whispered filthy words in her ear in that sexy voice.

She swallowed. "I feel like I'm speaking on behalf of women everywhere when I say it's a damn shame you nixed the brogue. You're depriving us, and that kind of selfishness should really be outlawed."

"Is that so?" he asked, still adopting the accent. His hazel eyes twinkled, and he took a step toward her, closing the distance between them.

It was the first time since finding him that she felt like she was actually talking to *her* Finley. This was familiar. This playful back and forth. Distantly she was aware that they didn't have time for a distraction, but she was a moth to a flame. Completely helpless to resist its pull.

Her tongue darted out, wetting her lips. "Definitely."

He traced the shell of her ear with his fingertips, and the electric buzz it shot through her went straight for her clit. He dipped his head, and her heart stuttered, thinking perhaps he was leaning in to kiss her. But then he started talking, and her knees damn near buckled from the shock.

"My God, lass, your perfect fucking arse makes me wish I could show you what the term kiltlifter really means."

"Jesus, fuck, tell me you have a spare kilt in your back pocket."

"Liked the sound of that, did ya?" He pulled away, a low laugh rumbling out of him as he stared down at her. "Aye, she likes it."

Quinn had to blink a few times to shake off the sexual fog he'd wrapped them in. Her snappy retort was loaded and ready to go, but she was so fucking tired of talking. Instead, she grasped two fistfuls of his shirt and yanked him to her, lifting up on her toes so his mouth crashed into hers.

There was no indecision on his part. No second's hesitation. When his lips found hers, it wasn't anything as simple as a kiss.

It was a complete fucking claiming—and it felt like coming home.

Quinn groaned into his mouth, tears pricking the back of her eyes. She never wanted to be anywhere else but here. Right here. In his arms. Breathing him in.

Finley ran his hands down her back until he was palming her ass and pressing her into his body. Before she could do more than register the swell of him, thick and solid against her belly, there was a terrible crack.

That was the only warning before they were flung apart, the ground quaking so hard it was impossible to get back to her feet. It all happened so fast, there wasn't time for her to do more than open her mouth in a stunned gasp as the sky split straight down the middle, tearing the street in two as easily as a photograph. Leaving her on one side and Finley on the other.

"Quinn," he roared, teasing accent abandoned in the wake of his terror. His eyes were crystal clear, his face twisted in desperate intent.

*Why is it we only seem to be screaming each other's names when one or both of us is about to die?*

Her heart simultaneously soared and shattered as he reached for her. *He remembers me.* Really *remembers me.* She held on to that truth, savoring the sweetness of it.

But it was too little, too late.

When they'd kissed, it must have magnified the effect of their earlier moments of contact, finally piercing the veil cutting Finley off from her. Unfortunately, the magic imprisoning him was sentient enough to realize it had been infiltrated, and it hadn't wasted any time striking back hard and fast.

Quinn was helpless to do anything but cry out his name as Finley was sucked into a swirling black vortex, vanishing from sight. The ground ceased its shaking the second he disappeared.

Anger and grief swirled in her chest as she staggered back to her feet, jaw clenched, hands fisted. It was obvious enough to her what had just happened. Sensing the threat she presented, the magic snatched him away, locking him up somewhere else in his mind.

Likely somewhere as far away from her as possible.

She'd only just started to undermine the spell's hold, but like any parasite, it clearly didn't want to relinquish control of its source. Which meant it was going to do everything in its power to maintain its chokehold on Finley.

But it was okay. She'd found him once; she'd do it again. Hell, she'd do it as many times as it took to get him free. This was only the first battle of what would surely be an all-out war.

Too bad for the spellcaster when they'd crafted this little trap of theirs, they'd had no way of accounting for *her.* She would undermine and unravel this stupid fucking spell thread by thread if she had to. Whatever it took, she'd use every dirty trick in her arsenal until she got what she'd come for. Quinn had no intention of giving up or playing nice.

In fact, she wasn't playing at all. This wasn't a game to her; it was life or death.

Finley belonged to her, and she would get him back. No supernatural agency, no woman, and certainly no puny display of magic would ever keep them apart.

He was hers.

And just like she'd told him before this madness started, she wasn't about to share.

# CHAPTER TEN
## FINLEY

There was a dreamlike quality to this place, and for several long seconds, he wasn't sure if he was awake or asleep. He couldn't recall how he'd gotten here, what he'd been doing immediately preceding his arrival. For all intents and purposes, he'd simply blinked and appeared.

He tilted his head back, staring at the sky with a quizzical frown. *Were skies supposed to look like this?* A rotating path of color set against iridescent clouds? The spiral itself drew his attention, nearly hypnotizing him with its slow, continuous rotation. Creating the sensation of falling into it, even though his feet were firmly planted on the ground.

Something shifted within the depths of the spiral, and he squinted, noting with mild surprise that it was not created out of solid color but a series of images. The pictures were distorted, stretching and twisting as they flickered in and out. But he did manage to make out something they all had in common.

Him.

These weren't random movie snippets. These were memories.

*His* memories.

As the realization struck him, the rest of the space took shape. Large white screens popped up as far as his eye could see. No, not screens. They weren't solid, as they would be if made from canvas. The substance was ephemeral, like clouds or early morning fog. It was just thick enough to create the illusion of a wall, but as he moved, so did they. Chasing and corralling him. Herding him.

Forcing him to walk in the direction they desired.

It was disturbing, his complete lack of control over himself. He was little more than a slave to the ever-evolving landscape around him. At the thought, he stopped, refusing to take another step against his will. He was only a puppet if he allowed it.

Unfortunately, he didn't recognize the true danger until it was too late. It was not following the path that put him at risk but standing still. When he stopped moving, tendrils of mist would detach from the clouds and latch onto him, sinking beneath the layers of his skin and coming to life, playing out in the theater of his mind.

Finley recoiled from the unwanted touch, which felt like the scrape of raw cotton over his skin, but he was already lost to the memory. His body tensed, prepared for the worst, but there was something infinitely comforting about the mental pictures taking shape.

And it wasn't just pictures.

All of his senses were activated. He could hear the soft crackle of a fire, smell the heady blend of leather, tobacco, and just a hint of rain.

Finley was interested in none of it.

His attention was wholly fixed on the old man sitting with a book spread open across his lap. It had been a long time since he had allowed himself to recall the man with deep brown eyes and faded orange hair. The green and blue plaid draped over his knees so worn it had felt like the downy tuft of a baby chick against Finley's young cheek.

He couldn't have been very old, maybe six or seven, and the man reading to him was his grandfather. This was after his mother had died, but before the old man had gotten sick, back when he still had a buffer between him and the Duke's rage.

Story time with his grandfather had been a welcome escape. A safe harbor in a world that grew more frightening every day. It's where Finley had discovered his love of learning and acquired his thirst for travel. He'd wanted to visit the far-off lands his grandfather spoke of. When you were a pirate or an explorer, it didn't matter who your father was, only how courageous you were. Names were what you made them—what you earned—not something you were born with.

Could there be anything more alluring to a boy who'd grown to despise his own?

It was part of the reason he'd so easily left his surname behind and taken on a pseudonym when he joined the Brotherhood. The boy he'd been didn't matter. Only the man he'd become.

This memory contained everything Finley loved about his childhood, and consequently, all the things that hurt him the most to remember once they'd been taken away. Which was why he'd refused to dwell on them.

Chest burning with age-old grief, he blinked away the memory, finding himself back beneath the swirling sky with its flickering images. Within seconds more tendrils broke free, and he started walking, determined not to fall victim to the images they contained.

He moved quickly but carefully, eyes on the lookout as the barriers on either side of him glided across the floor, blocking his way only to lay out a new path for him to follow. The deeper into this strange maze he traveled, the more aggressive the walls with their wisps of smoke became. Like he was an image they wanted to collect.

Finley started to walk faster, not sure where he was going or what he was searching for, only that what he wanted was away from this place. He had nothing to go on. Not a picture, not a name, just an intense certainty that he wasn't supposed to be here, that there was someone he needed to find.

He was so focused on his task he didn't realize until it was too late that he was heading for another one of the iridescent screens. He collided with it, but instead of bouncing off like he would a real wall, he passed straight through. Finley stepped out of the maze and straight into another animated set of images.

This one was all-encompassing. He wasn't just witnessing the memory; he was reliving it. The sky above was filled with roiling black clouds. Rain pelted down, so thick it was nearly blinding. The only light came from a series of spotlights scattered around what appeared to be a large warehouse.

He was running, heart thundering in his chest as he caught sight of a dark-haired woman with wine-colored eyes racing toward him. Her eyes were open wide, a spear clutched in her hand.

Finley glanced between her and the weapon, fear twisting his stomach into knots. He had the sudden urge to warn her about something. But before he could open his mouth, her face morphed, burning with deadly intent. In the same breath, she let go of the spear, sending it straight through him. He dropped to his knees, but she wasn't done with him yet.

Reaching up toward the sky, she took control of the storm. Calling down a bolt of lightning, she flung her hand back to him, sending the deadly energy into the metallic tip of the spear protruding from his torso. Molten lava surged through his veins as the electricity ran through him. After that, he knew only pain as he lay twitching on the ground, rain splashing into his eyes and mouth.

His consciousness faded, the world turning dark at the edges until he was no longer lying in the rain. He stood once more in the twisting nether of this mind palace, little wisps of smoke drifting off the bare skin of his forearms and rejoining the shimmering wall behind him.

Sweat broke out across his forehead as he struggled for control of his emotions. Even though he was free of the grisly memory, phantom pain echoed inside him. A chill settled deep into his muscles as if he was actually standing outside in the pouring rain.

But that wasn't what sent his heart racing.

There, just in the distance, he could make out a soft, rhythmic thud. Both familiar and terrifying.

Footsteps.

He was no longer alone.

Something about the sound niggled in the back of his mind, but there was no time to follow the thread to the warning his subconscious attempted to provide. Instinct roared at him to run.

So he did.

His pursuer gave chase, their steps picking up speed with every stride. Finley ran faster, sprinting until his throat was raw from the air he sucked deep into his lungs. He glanced over his shoulder to see if he could catch sight of who was coming for him, but there was no one there. His gut urged him not to believe that meant he was safe.

He was being hunted.

Finley continued to run, doing his best to avoid the pivoting walls as he followed the ever-evolving path. And then, finally, as he skidded around a corner, he caught sight of his shadow. His heart spasmed and his pulse roared in his ears.

It was *her*.

His murderer.

She must have come back to finish the job.

# CHAPTER ELEVEN
## QUINN

Holding her stilettos by the heels in one hand, she ran as fast as she could manage in her pencil skirt. It was marginally easier to keep pace with the footsteps ahead of her once she'd taken her shoes off, but the floor had an odd texture. It wasn't quite slick like tile, but it had a spongy quality that left a damp residue on her skin, causing her to slip every few steps.

"Dammit, Finley," she growled, turning a corner only to find it empty once again, "slow down and give a girl a chance, would ya? It's almost like you don't want to be caught."

She was well aware talking to him like this—like things were normal—was wholly for her benefit. Cora hadn't raised a fool. As soon as Quinn spied what was behind Door Number Two, she knew she'd be starting back at square one with him. But holding on to that shred of normalcy helped her stay sane. Which she was going to need if she had any chance of getting them both out of here in one piece.

Speaking of here . . .

Quinn eyed her new surroundings with supreme distrust. Either someone had slipped psychedelics into her tea while she hadn't been paying attention, or she'd just stepped through the looking glass. Though, Wonderland's brand of weird didn't hold a candle to the nausea-inducing sky and shifting cloud-walls in Finley's dreamscape. This place was fucked up with a capital F.

Despite all of that, a part of her was undeniably proud to note the disparity between the two locations. The London labyrinth had been the spell at its best. The showroom floor, if you will. This place was a far cry from that. There was something hurried and unpolished about it. Like it was raw code and not a full-fledged video game. All the bells and whistles were missing.

She took that as both a good sign and a warning. Good, because it meant she must have gotten close to breaking through. A warning because it meant that, like any cornered animal, the magic holding Fin here was going to lash out to defend itself.

Lungs burning, Quinn barreled forward. It wasn't until she was halfway down the new path that she realized the footsteps had faltered. If he stopped, this was her chance to catch up to him.

Tapping into a final burst of speed, Quinn silently vowed to buy Nord a mead distillery as thanks for insisting she join him and Lina for their morning workouts these last few months. If not for his relentless conditioning, there was no way she'd have lasted this long.

As she burst around the corner, she finally caught sight of Finley's chiseled profile. He turned to face her, his expression arrested as his eyes found hers. She slumped forward, shoes clattering to the floor as her hands braced on her thighs, supporting her as she gasped for breath.

"You're a real sonofabitch, you know that, Batman? It was like you ran faster when you heard me calling your name."

"Witch," he snarled, his voice laced with so much venom she jerked back up to a standing position.

"Excuse me?"

She blinked at him a couple of times in shock. This was a far different reception than she'd anticipated. She was expecting something more along the lines of his Dante reenactment from the labyrinth. Something that indicated his memory of her was missing. This level of vitriol was reserved for people—enemies—you knew. But if he remembered her, why would he think *she* was the enemy?

"I won't let you kill me again, witch."

"Kill you? You think I killed you?" She gestured at his very alive body. "But you're not even dead."

"I saw you with the spear, how you used your magic and called down the lightning to finish me off." The accusation in his voice struck her like a whip.

Her eyes narrowed, and her disbelief turned to exasperation. She reached forward and picked up one of her stilettos, hurling it at his head but missing him by several feet. In hindsight, it probably wasn't the best idea to attempt assault when trying to convince someone of her innocence, but she wasn't exactly thinking clearly.

"You faithless wanker! I'm not a witch, and that's not remotely what happened. I'll agree there was a spear, but I wasn't the one who hurled it at you. You nearly died trying to save me."

"That's not what I remember."

"You don't *remember* anything. It's just the spell trying to confuse you. Here, let me show you the truth." She held out her hand, taking a few steps closer.

He scrambled back, his eyes tightening. "Stay back, witch."

"Jesus, I'm going to get whiplash from your ever-changing opinion of me. First I'm an angel, and now I'm a witch. Sounds like some typical male patriarchy bullshit. As soon as you stop wanting to fuck me, you want to condemn me. Way to be part of the stereotype, Fin."

Something in his eyes flickered when she implied he wanted to fuck her, but his face twisted back into a scowl by the time she was done talking. "You're the one bringing up spells."

Quinn raked her fingers through her hair, squeezing the sides of her skull. "You are under a spell, asshole. I am the one trying to break it. What about that are you struggling to grasp? Spell, bad. Quinn, good. For fuck's sake, I think I liked you better when you were impersonating Dante."

"I don't like your tone."

That made her laugh. "Well, that's nothing new. From the day we've met, you've been more interested in what my mouth could do than the words coming out of it."

His brow creased, and for a second, her heart stopped its anxious beating because she thought he was going to refute the point. She used his momentary confusion to close the distance between them. When he finally realized she was close enough to touch him, he took two more hurried steps back.

"Come on, Finley. This isn't you. You've never run from anything a day in your life. Don't tell me you're scared of me."

"I'm not scared. I'm cautious. Which seems prudent considering I just watched you murder me."

"That's the most ridiculous thing I've ever heard. If ever there was a person you could trust, it's me. In fact, I'm probably the only person you can trust here."

He canted his head, eyes dark with suspicion. "You know where we are?"

"Uh, yeah, dipshit, we're in your head."

He glanced around. "This is a maze."

She pinched the bridge of her nose and let out a heavy sigh. "I'm not going to debate the philosophy of it with you. But you need to trust me."

"I have no reason to trust you."

"For the love of God, Finley. How many times do I have to tell you? I. Didn't. Kill. You." She knew her temper was showing on her face because heat crept into her cheeks, and Finley's gaze drifted down, noting it with interest.

Her tongue was always sharp, but it was rare she really let her emotions take control of her. She preferred to hide behind her barbed words and carefully constructed mask. It was safer there.

But safe wouldn't be enough. Not in here. Not with him.

Taking a deep breath, she lifted her hand. He jerked away once more, and she rolled her eyes. "I'm not going to touch you, even though it would make things a lot easier for us both if you would just nut up and let me."

"If you're not trying to touch me, what are you doing?"

"I'm just going to return something you lost."

He scoffed. "What could you possibly have that belongs to me?"

"A memory."

"How? If it's mine, how could you possess it?"

"Because I was there, Finley. But, more than that, when it comes to you, I know everything."

"I find that hard to believe." He crossed his arms and looked away, but he wasn't fooling her. She knew she'd piqued his interest, so she pushed on.

"I know how you take your tea—two tea bags because you're insane, milk second, no sugar. And how you fold your socks in half, like a freak, and then arrange them by color *and* pattern. Same as your shirts. I know your favorite color is purple. But not just any purple, deep plummy purple. And that you secretly love to sing when you think no one's listening. I know why cars are your first and true love. Not only are they your escape, they give you freedom. The ability to fuck off wherever you want as fast as you want, leaving everything and everyone behind."

Quinn wasn't sure when it started, but her voice was husky with unshed tears. And still she kept going, needing him to hear this, to believe her.

"I know you have a never-ending need for control. That you're rigid, infuriating, impossibly demanding, but also the most compassionate and giving man I've ever known. That you would rather die than see someone you care about—someone you love—suffer. That the one thing you crave most in this world is someone who would do the same for you."

"You can't possibly know all that."

He could deny it, but she knew she had him. She could see it in the frantic throb of the vein on the side of his neck. The slight widening of his eyes and the way he swayed forward as if unconsciously trying to get closer to her.

This time when she raised her hand, he didn't flinch. Not wanting to press her luck, she refrained from touching him, weaving her memory with the aid of compulsion and sending it to him.

He stiffened as it took hold, his eyes fluttering as they closed as if he was in the midst of an intense dream. It took five seconds, maybe ten, before they were open and peering into hers again.

"I can taste your tears," he whispered.

If she hadn't lived through that horrific battle herself, the words wouldn't have made sense. But since she'd spent her nights reliving every heart-wrenching second beginning with him screaming out for her right up until his body went limp on the pavement, she knew exactly what he was referring to.

"I told you I didn't kill you."

"But then why did I—"

"It's like I already said. It's the spell. It doesn't want you to trust me."

"And the spell is twisting my mind."

"Yes!"

"But you're in my mind. How do I know you're not part of the spell's magic?"

*Okay . . . that was a fair point.* All she could offer him was the truth, which, as far as explanations went, was pretty lacking.

"Because I am the one trying to help you see through the lies."

He frowned, clearly not buying it. "Why would my brain want to deceive me? Why should I trust you and not my own thoughts?"

"Because they aren't your thoughts. What reason do I have to lie to you, Finley? If I really was your enemy, why would you die trying to protect me?"

Without giving him a chance to reply, she crafted several similar memories. All times Finley had come to her rescue. All his declarations of intent. Both in word and in deed. The wyvern. Mataius. The stolen kiss in the alleyway. Their dance at Lina's reception. Their interrupted reunion and his promise it would never be over for them.

"Please stop," he begged, sucking in a harsh breath. Then he lifted both hands and pressed his fingers to his temples as if trying to relieve the pressure building there.

"Do you understand now?"

"No . . . I . . . I'm sorry, I want to. But it doesn't make sense."

Part of her wanted to throttle him. He was so goddamn stubborn he didn't want to believe what was right in front of him.

"You chose me, Finley. You've always chosen me. So choose me now. Trust me now. And if that's really too hard for you, then please, I'm begging you, trust yourself. Trust the man you really are. See past the lies. If not for me, then for yourself."

He looked at her, really looked at her, and for one wonderful moment, her brief flicker of hope turned into a full-on bonfire.

He started to open his mouth, and grief threatened to extinguish it entirely. She could feel his hesitation and the denial forming on his lips.

*Fuck.*

It wasn't enough. What she'd given back hadn't been enough. He needed more.

She needed to give him something else, something bigger. A moment initially experienced by him, so it was colored with his thoughts and emotions instead of hers.

To win him back, she'd have to return a piece of himself he didn't know she'd taken.

So she did.

# CHAPTER TWELVE
## FINLEY

*- The night after Lina's memories are restored -*

"*Don't come back tonight.*" Nord's growled command sounded in his mind as clearly as if the berserker was standing beside him.

Finley stiffened, his eyes flying to Quinn, who'd headed straight for her bar the second they'd stepped through the portal. She'd already pulled down two glasses and was at work uncorking an expensive bottle of cabernet.

"*Where am I—*"

"*Do. Not. Come. Home.*" Nord's clipped response left no room for argument. If Finley so much as tried to set foot in his penthouse, he was likely to lose said foot.

*Bloody hell.*

He took one look at the portal still pulsing beside him and snapped the tether, closing it. If he had to sleep on a couch, he might as well do it in the home of a beautiful—if maddening— woman instead of the far less attractive geezer they'd just left. No offense to Alistair.

"Mind if I crash here tonight?"

Quinn's eyes darted to him, something like panic flickering in the burgundy depths. He held her stare, struck again by the bewitching color of her irises. They were always a shade of reddish-purple, though depending on her mood, it might be more of one than the other. Sometimes aubergine, sometimes a deep plum, other times, like now, a near-perfect match for the wine in her stemless glass.

"I have it on good authority there's a perfectly good bed waiting for you in your penthouse."

"There is."

"So why stay here?"

He raised a brow, letting his silence answer for him.

"Oh, I see." She smirked to herself, seeming inordinately pleased at the thought of Nord and Lina requiring privacy. "Mission accomplished."

"What?"

She blinked. "Nothing. Wine?"

She poured him a glass before he could refuse, sauntering over to him with a seductive sway he'd come to learn was entirely natural. He wasn't even sure she knew she extended a carnal invitation with each step she took. Then again, everything she did was deliberate, so perhaps she did.

Quinn held the glass of wine out to him. He stared at it for a second, wishing it was scotch but knowing better than to say so. Everything was a test with this woman, and he was tired of failing. Instead, he accepted the drink with a smile he hoped didn't look like a grimace.

"Cheers."

She clinked her glass with his, returning his toast. "Cheers." Lifting the dark purple liquid to her lips, she took a deep swallow and made her way to the oversized sofa.

Finley's gaze dropped without permission, appreciating her delectable arse for several seconds before he cleared his throat and forced himself to look elsewhere. Without taking any of them in, his eyes moved over the dove gray furniture, the chrome and glass chandelier, and the stone feature wall. If asked to describe her flat later, the best he'd manage was that it was both expensive and feminine. Even looking away, he was far too focused on her to notice much of anything else.

When he finally allowed his eyes to drift back to her, they caught on the small, knowing smile playing about her luscious lips. He couldn't help but picture them wrapped around his shaft, her cheeks hollowing out as she sucked him deep. His cock gave an approving twitch, and he had to pretend to inspect the bookcase behind him to disguise the fact he was adjusting himself.

*Fucking Christ. Get ahold of yourself, mate.*

The woman had to be part succubus with the way his mind always seemed to stray toward sex in her company. It was bloody embarrassing. All she needed to do was look in his direction, and he started straining against his trousers.

Why had he thought sleeping here was the better alternative?

"Like what you see?"

Finley choked. The minx had waited until he'd taken a sip of his drink to ask her deceptively innocent question.

"It's lovely," he managed, turning back to face her.

There was no missing the laughter in her eyes. "It'd better be. I paid a pretty penny for it. Several, in fact. It took nearly six months for the contractors to fly in the slate for the fireplace."

She gestured to the wall he'd pretended to be admiring, but his gaze snagged on her long legs as she curled them beneath her. For some unknown reason, he was suddenly fascinated with the way the straps of her seven-inch stilettos wrapped up her calf. He wanted to trace the path with his tongue.

"Won't you join me? It's bad manners to make a lady drink alone." She leaned forward, patting the couch cushion beside her.

Finley was grateful he'd slid his free hand into his pocket while his back had been turned. At least now she wouldn't be able to immediately tell his cock was rock hard and aching.

How the hell was he supposed to sit that close to her without giving in to the need to touch her?

She was Lina's best friend. And the Satori heir. Quinn wasn't simply off-limits; she was so far out of reach she might as well be on a different fucking planet. Getting involved with her was the worst possible idea imaginable.

And yet it was all he could think about.

"You're not drinking alone," he said, taking another sip to prove his point and using the moment to steel his resolve. Glass nearly empty, Finley moved over to the couch, taking a seat on the opposite end, mirroring her position with his back resting against the arm of the chair, body angled toward her. "Better?"

She smirked. "I wouldn't go that far. If it was up to me, I would have spent the night getting nice and sweaty with some gorgeous stranger from The District, but . . ." She let the word hang, sipping her drink while staring at him coyly over the rim. "I suppose you'll have to do."

Finley objected to the implication that he was her second choice of companion for the evening. Even though it hadn't exactly been her choice at all to bring him home with her, his jealousy wasn't prepared to be logical about the matter. It rose hot and fast, causing a muscle to flutter in his jaw as he clenched it. "No one told you to blackmail the fae tosser. He's the one that kicked you out, not me."

She lifted one shoulder in a shrug, sending a wave of her inky black hair sliding across her creamy skin. Finley had the sudden urge to wrap it around his fist and yank. Hard.

"He had it coming."

"Seemed like it."

Her lips curled up. "Smart man agreeing with the scary lady."

"You don't scare me."

"Oh? Then why are you sitting all the way over there?"

Finley drained his glass. "It's comfortable."

Quinn shot him a looked filled with disbelief and then did the same with her wine. Glass empty, she lifted the bottle and gave them both a top-up.

"Are you trying to get me drunk, Satori?"

She flashed him a playful grin. "More like I'm trying to keep my buzz going."

He wondered if that was wise, but he was hardly in a position to question her on it. She must have sensed it too, because she practically dared him to say something.

Deciding silence was safer, he let his eyes wander again, nursing his drink as he noted the lack of personal effects. Other than a lone picture on the mantel, the only other non-essential object in the room was a single candle on the coffee table. The latter was clearly there for convenience rather than decoration.

"So . . . lived here long?"

"Is that really the best you can do?"

"Pardon?"

She let out a long-suffering sigh. "I'm not one for boring small talk, 007. If you're going to interrogate me, at least make it interesting."

"Interesting?"

"Strip back the layers. Make it hurt."

For the second time that night, Finley nearly choked on his wine. She couldn't possibly have meant for that to come out as suggestively as it had. As if she was asking him for something else entirely, something he was suddenly desperate to give her. Pleasure predicated by the sharp bite of pain.

His hand curled reflexively as if wrapping around the handle of one of the leather-bound implements in the back of his closet.

*Fuck.*

"Here. I'll make it easy for you." She chugged her nearly full glass and stood, moving back toward her bar to pull out a familiar amber-filled bottle. "You're a Macallan man, right?"

Finley nodded, sensing where this was going and dreading it as much as he wanted it to play out.

"Good, because if you were going to say you preferred something pedestrian like Johnny Walker, I was going to have to insist you leave."

"You're a bit of a snob, Satori."

"I am French after all—on my father's side," she added, answering the question before he had a chance to voice it. "I have a reputation to uphold. Besides, it takes one to know one."

Finley's lips hitched. He made no claims otherwise. He liked expensive, beautiful things. Nothing wrong with that.

She stared at the cabernet he'd barely touched. "Finish that."

"You're bossy too."

This time it was her lips that lifted as she repeated herself. "Takes one to know one."

*Did she mean . . .*

Finley shook off the thought, knowing he was already in dangerous territory. Courting ideas like that would end badly. If only because he'd want to take the bait and prove his dominance.

Lifting the glass, he held her gaze as he drained it.

"Good boy."

Fuck if that didn't make his dick twitch.

Never in his centuries-long life had he been turned on by the thought of ceding the upper hand to a potential lover. But Quinn hadn't asked him to; she'd simply taken it. As if it was her right.

His palm itched with the need to correct her assumption. Even as a quiet part of himself wanted to find out what it would be like to put himself at her mercy. Would she tame him? *Could* she?

Dangerous territory indeed.

Quinn Satori had just become more than a temptation. She was a challenge . . . and Finley never backed down from a challenge.

"There are only two rules to this game."

Finley blinked, realizing he'd gotten lost in his wandering

thoughts. Quinn had set the open bottle of scotch between them on the coffee table and reclaimed her seat across from him.

"We take turns asking the other a question. You either answer the question, or you take a drink. Simple."

The thought of drinking the expensive alcohol straight from the bottle pained him. It was disrespectful. But this was her game, and she'd set the rules. He'd follow them.

For now.

"Who goes first?" he asked.

She waved her hand in his direction. "But make it good, Fin, because when it's my turn, I'm not pulling any punches."

With his mind so deeply in the gutter, it didn't take him long to come up with something. Depending on how the night played out, he might need to make use of her answer come the morning.

"What's your favorite breakfast?"

Her eyes sparkled with mischief, and he knew he was in trouble before the answer left her lips. "In a perfect world, a nice lazy fuck with my partner from the night before. But if you're asking about food . . . French toast. Powdered sugar and strawberries, no syrup." She leaned forward with a grin. "My turn. Are you a top or a bottom?"

"Top." His answer was firm. He hadn't even blinked before providing it.

Color pinkened her smooth cheeks. "Are you sure?"

"Unequivocally."

She raised a brow. "You don't know what you're missing then."

"That was two questions," he said, not acknowledging her assessment.

She huffed but gestured for him to go.

"Shower or bath?"

"Am I alone?"

"Yes."

"Bath. My turn. Blondes or brunettes?"

"Brunettes. Though recently I've discovered a preference for jet black."

She tried to hide her reaction, but his attention was laser-focused on her, so there was no missing the heat flaring to life in her eyes. His next question fell out without conscious thought.

"What's the worst thing you've ever done?"

She straightened, hand reaching for the bottle before she hesitated, took a deep breath, and looked back at him. "Fall in love. How old were you when you lost your virginity?"

"Twenty-four."

Her jaw dropped. "Twenty. Four. How ever did you hold off for so long? A handsome chap like you, surely there were offers . . ."

"Is that a question?"

She shook her head. "Just a musing."

"What's the longest you've gone without sex?"

Quinn blinked. "Recently? A couple months. You?"

"You still owe me another answer."

"Fine. What's your next question then?"

"Why do you prefer one-night stands instead of meaningful relationships?"

She hadn't been expecting that one. He could see the flash of vulnerability in the back of her eyes. Instead of answering, Quinn lifted the bottle of scotch and swallowed once . . . twice. Finley watched the delicate column of her throat as it worked, his mind taking a decidedly dirty turn once again.

Her cheeks were flushed from the drink, and he had to bite back a groan when her tongue darted out to catch a drop of the amber liquid from her lips.

*Tease.*

"What's your safe word?"

She was trying to surprise a reaction out of him with her questions. He wasn't about to give her one. Instead, Finley forced his body to retain its relaxed position, cheek resting on the fist of one hand, his other curled around the ankle propped on his knee. "I've never needed one."

Her eyes narrowed with disappointment. "That's not an answer. If you were to pick one, what would it be?"

He wanted to point out she was breaking her own rules by continuing to ask multiple questions in a row, but he'd give her this one. "Aubergine."

She sputtered. "Like the penis emoji?"

*Like the color of your eyes.* But he didn't correct her. He opted for an enigmatic smile instead.

"You must really like eggplants," she muttered with a slight shake of her head.

"It's my favorite color," he corrected, not giving her a chance to comment before asking his next question. "What's yours?"

"Snow."

No hesitation. She wanted him to know.

*Interesting.*

This evening had taken an unexpected turn, though he couldn't deny he was enjoying it.

She tapped a finger to her lip, her eyes narrowed thoughtfully. "Choices, choices. Okay, I know. How long has it been since you've been with someone?"

"Sex or a relationship?"

"Is there a difference?"

"For me? Yes."

"Okay . . . sex then."

"Two years."

Quinn's eyes went wide. "You haven't had sex in two *years*?"

"No."

"Are you celibate or something?"

"Selective."

The kind of arrangements he preferred demanded it. Casual sex held no appeal to him. He needed to know his partners in order to give them pleasure. That took time. Intimacy. He didn't like to rush into it.

"What about a relationship?" Quinn asked, dropping all pretense of their game.

He toyed with the idea of not answering but didn't see the harm. "Nearly a decade since my last."

Her jaw dropped. "A *decade*? Christ . . . " Her eyes dropped to his pants. "Please tell me you at least wank off regularly. It's not natural to deny yourself like that."

"Was that a question?"

But she wasn't listening. She glanced away, holding a quiet one-sided conversation with herself. "Jesus, the next time you come . . . it's going to be fucking life-altering. The best you've ever had . . ."

She pinned him with a look, and he suddenly felt like he was caught in the middle of a spider's web.

Shit.

Quinn wasn't one to back down from a challenge either, and by telling her how long he'd abstained, he'd just wrapped himself in a fucking bow as far as she was concerned.

He could see it in her eyes.

Quinn Satori was going to seduce him.

Everything up until that point had been child's play compared to what she had in store for him now that she was pulling out the big guns.

He was so fucking screwed.

Without saying a word, she lifted the scotch and drank deep, then held it out to him. He eyed her warily but accepted it, a small thrill running through him as his lips closed around the bottle just where hers had been seconds prior. The smoky alcohol burned a path down his throat and sent warmth radiating out from his chest.

While he was busy setting the bottle down, she crawled over to him, lifting up on her knees once she reached him and then sliding forward to straddle his lap.

Finley forgot how to breathe. "What are you doing?"

"What does it look like I'm doing?" she asked, hands at work on his tie.

He captured her wrist, halting her in the act of pulling it free. Before he could speak, she leaned forward, slowly licking the seam of his mouth with just the tip of her tongue and sending a bolt of lust spearing straight through him. She tasted like smoke and honey. Decadent. Heady.

Forbidden.

She cradled his face in her hands, running her nose along the length of his before taking his bottom lip between her teeth and biting down gently. She released him and pulled back just enough to demand, "Kiss me."

"I can't," he managed, his voice a strangled whisper.

"You poor dear. It's been so long you've forgotten. Here, let me show you."

She leaned into him, rolling her hips over his straining erection as she feathered her lips against his. It was barely a kiss, but it had him panting with the need for more. It took every ounce of his control to remain completely still.

"No, silly, you don't just sit there." She used one hand to squeeze his cheeks, forcing him to pucker. Lips against his, she breathed, "You have to kiss. Me. Back."

Finley lost the battle as she licked into his mouth, helpless not to respond.

"Yes," she groaned, rocking against his throbbing cock once more. "Just like that."

He'd been riding the edge most of the night, and just that single act of friction was enough to make him worry about creaming his trousers.

She ran her free hand down his torso, slipping buttons free and sliding his shirt open so her smooth palm could glide unobstructed down his feverish skin. He could hardly think straight. It wasn't until she reached for his belt that he snapped back to himself.

"Aubergine."

Quinn froze, leaning back with a look of utter shock on her face. "W-what?"

"I can't. Not with you. Not like this."

It was the absolute worst fucking thing he could have said, and he instantly berated himself as she jumped off him.

"I'm sorry, I must have misread the situation."

She was already halfway across the room. He'd seen people flee a fire with less haste.

"No, fuck. Quinn, just wait a damn minute, will you?"

She stopped, her body rigid as she glanced back at him over her shoulder.

"It's not that I don't want you. You know I fucking do. But you're Lina's best friend. And a Satori. I can't do casual with you."

She held his gaze, her chest rising and falling rapidly. He held his breath, waiting for the condemnation he was sure she was about to level him with. But when she finally answered, her words were hollow, her expression haunted.

"And I don't do serious."

He nodded, chest tight. That was the crux of it. He'd throw away every bloody rule he'd ever followed if he thought there was a chance this could mean as much to her as it would to him. But he wouldn't put his heart on the line for someone who saw him as something to be conquered.

He wanted more than that—especially from her.

One night would never be enough for him.

Quinn sighed, her body losing some of its tension. "I understand. Thank you for stopping me before I made a mistake we'd both regret."

She might understand, but the coolness of her tone told him she hadn't forgiven him. Not even close.

"I'll just go get you a blanket and some pillows."

He watched her disappear down the hall until he couldn't see her, and then he dropped his head to his hands, letting out a low groan.

*Stupid fucking git, she's never going to trust you now. Couldn't you find a way to stop things without completely fucking embarrassing her? Christ, you're bloody useless.*

He didn't hear her come back into the room. He was too deep in his mental self-flagellation to make out her footsteps creeping up behind him. The last thing he recalled was a warm palm sliding over his shoulder and a few whispered words in his ear.

"When you wake up, the only thing you'll remember about spending the night is that you slept on the couch."

# CHAPTER THIRTEEN
## QUINN

She waited with bated breath for the memory to release him. There were a lot of ways the next handful of minutes could go, and she'd considered all of them plenty of times. Though, in her musings, Finley hadn't been simultaneously suffering the effects of a mind-shattering spell. It was too soon to tell if that was going to work out to her benefit.

She felt sick from the onslaught of adrenaline. Her heart raced, her breaths were too shallow, her legs felt as if they might give out any second. He might be the one reliving the stolen moment, but she was willing to bet she was the one suffering.

The wait for his reaction was agony, and yet it was still over too quickly.

Far sooner than she expected, Finley sucked in a shuddering breath and blinked once, slowly. When his eyes found hers, there was accusation, anger, frustration, disbelief, and most surprisingly, desire.

"Why?"

The lone word was half-bitten off, half-snarled. For a second, he almost reminded her of Nord. Like the proof of her manipulation had set something wild loose inside of him.

Quinn swallowed back a wave of nausea, prepared for this question, even if her honesty now was late, at best.

"I was embarrassed."

For someone who prided herself on not abusing her gift, she was certainly quick to bust it out when it suited her, regardless of what someone else might have to say about the matter. She'd always rationalized it by telling herself that they wouldn't remember, so what was the harm?

But the harm was standing right across from her, staring her in the face. Because shining brighter than all the other emotions warring for dominance was hurt. She hadn't just hurt him; she'd gutted him.

"Fin, I'm sorry."

"You didn't trust me enough to even let me remember what transpired between us?"

The question hit a little too close to home. This wasn't even the worst of what she'd taken from him. And witnessing the depth of his reaction to the 'lesser evil' was not exactly filling her with the warm and fuzzies for how he'd react when he learned the whole truth.

Worried her plan to save him was backfiring, and that she might have just pushed him away instead of bringing him back, Quinn started talking, her words a hurried jumble.

"You saw what happened. I made a complete ass of myself. I'd been drinking all night and was lonely, and you were right there looking like you'd been ripped straight out of my dirtiest fantasies. All reserved and . . . and British. You have this coiled sensuality about you, and I wanted to see what happened if I could get under your skin and set it free. And I . . . I don't have a good excuse, okay? My defenses were down, and I just went for it. Fuck, Fin, you must know how much I want you. How badly I've always wanted you, even if I've been too much of a chickenshit to admit it to anyone, least of all myself."

He looked conflicted, like he wanted desperately to believe her, but something was holding him back.

"If you felt that way, why run? All you had to do was say it could be more than one night, and I would have caved. I would have given you everything."

"That's exactly what sent me running, Batman. You were demanding strings, and I was terrified of being tied to anyone."

"And you still are."

The words broke her heart. Not because they were wrong or because he sounded so fucking dejected, but because they proved that she was failing. The memory hadn't been enough to pull him back together. He was reacting to the reminder of what she'd shown him, riding the lingering emotions. But he still didn't remember her . . . *them.* Not completely. If he did, he'd never need to ask the question.

Fuck, her mother had been right.

She couldn't hold anything back. It had to be all or nothing.

She'd been holding off, saving this final piece as a last-ditch attempt. Because if returning it didn't work, nothing would. He would be lost to her forever, and her heart wouldn't survive the loss.

Sucking in a breath, she forced herself to meet his gaze. "Do you at least trust me now? That I'm telling you the truth when I say I'm here to help you and I would never have tried to kill you?"

"How can I trust you? All you've proven is that you'll do anything to protect yourself, including hurt someone you claim to care about."

The blow landed, far harder than he'd probably intended. Because he was speaking of her behavior in the past, but the statement was true even now. She'd never had an issue walking the morally gray path to protect the people she loved—including herself. And it was all coming around to bite her in the ass right now, when she was desperately trying to save the one person who'd come to mean more to her than any other.

"Maybe that's true, but I owned up to it when I didn't have to. That has to count for something."

"You don't get to play God with someone's mind and then bully them into forgiveness after the fact. You had no right to steal that memory from me."

Quinn bowed her head, accepting the blame as her due. She'd known this was a possibility, and his anger was far easier to bear than his pain.

When she glanced back up, his eyes were narrowed and filled with suspicion. "What else have you taken?"

Quinn bit her lip, knowing it was now or never. That truth was the only thing that would set her—and him—free.

"Let me show you."

# CHAPTER FOURTEEN
## FINLEY

*- Two years before Lina's return -*

Auction night at The District was a necessary evil. At least one Guardian always attended to keep tabs on what was for sale and who bid on what, and tonight, he'd drawn the short straw.

Finley didn't mind pulling out his tux and dressing for the occasion or even slumming it with what constituted the supernatural demimonde. But he did object to the obligation infringing on his other, more intimate pursuits.

He moved around the outside of the main room, making note of tonight's patrons and trying his best to blend in.

"Cocktail, monsieur?" A pretty blonde gave him a bold smile, holding out a tray laden with a dozen fizzy red drinks.

"What is it?" he asked as he accepted one from the scantily clad server.

"A vampire's kiss."

"Sounds dangerous."

She flashed him a little fang. "Only in the wrong hands."

"Good to know."

She leaned into him, the scent of something noxiously floral filling his nose and making him want to sneeze. "Can I get you anything else? We have all manner of devilish delights on the menu tonight."

Finley smiled politely, if coolly, at the blatant invitation in her eyes. "No, thank you. I'm all set."

"My name's Nicolette. Let me know if you change your mind."

He gave her a noncommittal nod, pulling a balled-up cocktail napkin out of his pocket as she walked away. He eyed the phone number she'd scrawled on it with a sigh.

"I'd chuck that if I were you."

The husky voice came from behind him to the left. He glanced over his shoulder, feeling like he'd been struck by lightning as he stared at the dark-haired angel standing there smirking at him.

She was an absolute vision in scarlet, her gown the same vibrant shade as her painted lips. The bold color was a stunning contrast to the pale perfection of her skin and her midnight-colored hair, which she'd left in a simple but elegant plait over her shoulder. The silk dress was a tease, the plunging neckline and hip-high slit showing off as much skin as they concealed.

Suddenly the night's assignment didn't seem like such a loss. He vowed then and there to learn everything he could about this gorgeous creature.

Finley lifted his gaze, drinking her in while simultaneously trying to memorize as many details as he could. The longer he studied her, the stronger his urge to take off his jacket and wrap her up. He was not a jealous person by nature, but he was certainly feeling territorial right now. He didn't want anyone to feast on her beauty but him.

And then their eyes finally met.

The sense of knowing was so intense his blood practically sizzled with it. His pulse roared in his ears, and his knees nearly went out from beneath him.

*Purpose.*

*Your purpose.*

*She. Is. Yours.*

Finley's throat went dry, and he was pretty fucking sure his heart stopped beating. He never, not in a million years, thought he'd be one of the lucky ones. One of the few members of the Brotherhood to find the reason for their existence, the lone person they were soul-bound to serve and protect.

His mind emptied save for a single warning rolling through it on a loop.

*Don't fuck this up. Don't fuck this up.*

*Do. Not. Fuck. This. Up.*

She was looking at him quizzically, her head tilted to the side, and he realized he'd been standing there staring at her like a daft tosser.

It took him a moment to remember how to speak. "You think I should chuck the number?"

"The drink. I'm pretty sure *Nicolette* put something in it. She hasn't stopped eye-fucking you since she clocked you walking in." There was an appreciative pause as she gave him a slow once-over. "Not that I blame her."

"And you are?"

"Does it matter?"

*More than you could ever know.*

"I think it does."

"If a name is that important to you, you may call me Leona."

He knew it was an alias the second it left her lips. Though he was more interested in *why* she felt the need for secrecy. Instinctively, he searched the crowd around them, wondering if one of the guests could be a potential threat. Lucky for her, she had him now, which meant she'd never need to fear for her safety again. Not so long as he drew breath.

She couldn't possibly know what it meant to belong to a Guardian, and this was hardly the place to make such a declaration, so he'd allow her to hide behind her pseudonym. At least while they remained at The District.

Once they were alone, however, he'd demand her true name. And the rest of her secrets. He'd strip them all from her as surely as he would that dress. By the time the first rays of sunlight shot across the sky, he'd know every single inch of her.

Taking a step closer, he took her gloved hand in his and bowed so he could press a kiss to the back of it. He was already so attuned to her he caught the slight shiver the brush of his lips sent rushing up her arm.

"Pleasure to meet you, Leona." *I'm yours.* "I'm Finley."

"The pleasure's all mine."

*Not yet, but it's about to be.*

He held her hand in his longer than was probably acceptable, but now that he was touching her, he didn't want to stop. He released her with a sigh, already looking for a reason he could touch her again. His eyes landed on the dance floor. Without permission, his lip curled in distaste. He wasn't a fan of the modern practice of dry humping strangers to a beat and calling it dancing. Where was the art? The sense of discipline?

"You a big dancer?" she asked, the slight laugh in her voice indicating she'd picked up on his disdain.

"When the occasion calls for it."

"And does it?"

"That depends. Are you asking me to dance?"

"Definitely not. I'm a lady. My mother taught me to wait for a proper invitation."

"You don't strike me as a rule follower."

She snickered. "That obvious, huh?"

"Only to someone paying attention."

Her gaze, which had followed his to the dance floor, flicked back up to him. There was no mistaking the slight hitch in her breath or the interest blazing in her eyes. "I can follow rules."

The words went straight to his dick. She couldn't have made that sound more erotic if she'd tried. For a man who sought out control in nearly every situation, it was the equivalent of a red flag being waved at a bull.

"Is that so?"

"When the occasion calls for it."

God, she was perfect.

He loved that she'd taken his words and flung them right back at him. That she was as playful as she was sexy. That both versions of her were utterly without artifice. He had no illusions that she'd make things easy on him. If anything, she'd likely make him work for every single inch, and he couldn't fucking wait.

This was the most fun he'd had in . . . well, ever. Unless he was test-driving a potential new member of his automotive harem, fun wasn't exactly a word in his repertoire. Life hadn't prepared him for fun. But he was going to make up for it now. With her.

It had only just begun, and already he never wanted this night to end.

Thank God they had forever.

"May I have this dance?" He stood with one arm behind his back, the other held out to her in invitation.

She bit down on her lip and glanced between his hand and back out at the grinding bodies. "Maybe somewhere more private?"

Finley swallowed a groan. He had every intention of taking her home, but not yet. They only got one first night together; he wanted it to be perfect. She deserved for it to be more than a mad dash to the bedroom, even if that's exactly what his body was screaming for him to do.

He glanced around, spotting a nearby alcove.

"Give me just a second. I'll be right back."

She opened her mouth to protest, but he was already moving.

Without warning, he peeled back the velvet curtain separating the quiet little pocket from the rest of the room.

"What the hell do you think you're doing?" a shifter on the receiving end of an enthusiastic blow job snarled. The woman on her knees before him tried to sit up, but the shifter kept his hands curled in her hair, holding her down.

Finley pulled out a billfold, not bothering to count the money before he held it out. "Go somewhere else."

"Excuse me?" the wolf snarled.

Finley tossed the cash beside him on the leather couch. His eyes went wide when he saw the stack of bills.

"Come on, sweetheart. Let's take this party upstairs."

The couple left in a hurry. The semi-circular couch and round table appeared clean, but he hailed a nearby server anyway. "Can I get a cleanup and some champagne, please?"

"Right away, sir," the pixie murmured, her wings shooting off a little flurry of sparkles as she rushed to do his bidding.

His prize stood with her arms across her chest, an amused smile curling her lips. "Impressive."

Finley shrugged. "My lady requested privacy. I aim to please."

"And do you always get what you want?" she asked, moving to join him.

"Always."

She paused beside him, reaching out to adjust his bowtie. She hummed softly in her throat. "So do I."

"Of that, I have no doubt, princess."

She cocked a brow. "What happened to using my name?"

*It's not your real name, and I only want the truth between us.*

"I think princess suits you better."

"And you know me well enough already to have come to that conclusion, have you?"

"Well enough? Not remotely. But enough to know that much."

"You're good."

*Oh, sweetheart. You have no fucking idea how good I can be.*

The pixie returned with their bottle of champagne and used her magic to give the small space a quick tidy. Finley discreetly passed her a tip, leaning over to make one last request in her ear.

She grinned and gave him an almost imperceptible nod before rushing off.

"What was that about?"

"You'll see," he promised, placing his hand on the bare skin of her back to usher his date forward. "After you."

She took two steps forward and then paused, looking up at him. "Why do I get the feeling you're trying to sweep me off my feet?"

He grinned. "Doesn't every princess deserve to be properly courted?"

Color tinged her cheeks, and the blush made her look surprisingly vulnerable. She cleared her throat. "I don't trust stories that promise a happily ever after."

"That's only because it hasn't happened for you yet."

"I think you've got the wrong idea. I'm not looking for my Prince Charming, handsome."

"Good, because I might be charming, but I'm far from a prince."

Her brows lifted, and she peered into his eyes as if by doing so, she could see into his soul. "Accent. Money. Manners. Could have fooled me."

"Mere window-dressing." He leaned down so his mouth was just beside her ear. "I've always fancied myself a bit of a rake."

More color suffused her skin, this time her flush settling on her chest. "Oh, really?"

"Princes have to do what they're told. Rakes take what they want. When they want. Without apology."

"And what is it you want, Finley?"

"You."

Her breath caught, and this time there was no hesitation when she leaned into him. "Then take me."

"I intend to."

"What's stopping you?"

"Nothing."

She gestured to the debauchery in full swing around them. "And yet, we're still here."

"You wanted to dance."

"There are lots of ways to dance, handsome. Not all of them require a crowd, or clothes for that matter."

"Be that as it may, I have a plan. Stop trying to take the reins and let me execute it."

A surprised laugh escaped her. "I'm not used to people telling me no."

"Neither am I."

She breezed past him into the alcove, lifting one of the two glasses of bubbly. "One of us is going to have to learn to compromise, you know."

"I haven't started yet, love. So I guess you better get used to it."

"Tougher men than you have tried to tame me."

"Perhaps they lacked my motivation." He joined her, lifting his own glass and holding it out to her in a salute. "But you're wrong about one thing."

"What's that?"

He drained his glass, the bubbles tickling his throat as he made her wait for the answer. "I don't want to tame you."

Her throat bobbed. "You don't?"

He gave her a slow shake of his head as he set both their glasses back on the table. "No, princess. I want to set you free."

She pressed her hand to her chest. "Fuck me, you're swoony."

"I'm only just getting started."

"That's what I'm worried about," she admitted, sounding thoroughly put out by the idea.

He laughed and swept her up in his arms, the soft strains of an orchestra draining out all the nose from the club's main room as they started to dance in the privacy of their personal ballroom.

"Where's the music coming from?" she asked, craning her neck as if in search of hidden speakers or musicians.

"Shh," he whispered, holding her tighter and loving the way she perfectly fit against him. As if she'd been made for him . . . because she had. "Just follow my lead."

She stiffened in his arms, her voice almost too low for him to make out. "I'm afraid."

"Of what?" He pulled back to look at her face, but she stubbornly ducked her chin and laid her cheek against his shoulder.

She forced out a laugh, her voice deceptively breezy. "Of you stepping on my toes."

He knew she was covering up an accidental slip, that she hadn't intended to reveal any true vulnerability. But that was okay. Before the night was through, he'd show her she had nothing to fear. Not with him.

They danced, one song bleeding into the next, their bodies moving together as if they'd done it a thousand times before. Finally, when he couldn't stand the thought of denying them any longer, he tipped her chin up with his finger.

"Come home with me."

"I thought you'd never ask."

# CHAPTER FIFTEEN
## FINLEY

*- A little later that same night -*

"You live here by yourself?"

He shut the door to the penthouse and moved to help the enchanting woman whose real name he still didn't know out of her coat. "You sound surprised."

"It's just a lot of house for a bachelor."

"I like space."

"I can see that."

"So far all you've seen is the hallway."

"It's a *really* big hallway."

Finley laughed as he hung up her coat. "Would you like the rest of the tour, or—"

"Or."

He turned around, hands in his pockets as he looked at her. "If I didn't know better, I'd say you were in a hurry."

She walked over to him, resting her hands against his chest as she leaned in close. "I've been waiting all night for 'or.' And Finley?"

"Hmm?"

"I'm done waiting."

She rocked up, her lips coming straight for his. He turned his face just in the nick of time, causing her lips to meet his cheek. Before she could jerk back, he caught her with one hand around her wrist, holding her in place.

"I decide when you've had enough."

A barely audible whimper escaped her.

"Give me your name."

"I already—"

"Your *real* name, princess."

She leaned her head back, staring up at him with furrowed brows. "Why do you care so much?"

"I insist on knowing the name of the woman I'm going to spend the rest of the night fucking."

"That's ambitious."

"That's the truth."

She swallowed, her eyes glittering with arousal.

He trailed the tip of one finger from her collarbone down the line of her cleavage. "If all goes according to plan, you're about to be naked, spread wide, and dripping in my bed."

"Is that all?" She was trying for unaffected, but the breathless rasp of her voice gave her away.

Finley dipped his head so that his lips hovered just above hers. "That's just the beginning. Give me your name, and I'll show you the rest."

"Kiss me first."

He had to admire her nerve, his sulky, petulant little brat. But he was a patient man. He'd waited this long to have her. What were a few minutes more?

"No."

"Fuck you."

"No, sweetheart, I'm going to fuck *you*. Now, give me what I want, so I can give us what we both need."

"Keep talking like that, and I won't need you to do anything. I'll come right here in your big-ass hallway."

"Wrong again, princess. When you come, and I promise you will, it's going to be in my bed with my cock buried inside you and my name on your lips. I want the same privilege."

"Fuck," she whispered.

He hooked his finger into the silk of her dress so it was nestled between her breasts as she drew in a deep breath.

"Give. Me. Your. Name."

He yanked his arm back, pulling her forward so that she toppled into him, thrown completely off-balance.

"It's Quinn, you bastard."

His lips captured hers before she was finished speaking. A low rumble sounded deep in his throat as her mouth opened up beneath his. She tasted like fucking sin. Champagne and just a hint of strawberry. He could devour her if she let him.

One hand was still fisted in his shirt. The other scraped down his scalp, pulling his head closer to hers.

She was intoxicating. His favorite indulgence. If he wasn't careful, he'd get carried away right here, and he'd break his first promise to her.

Nipping her bottom lip, he brought the kiss to an end.

"Was that so hard?"

"Harder than I care to explain," she muttered, eyes hooded. Her words were purposely vague, and he didn't like what they hinted at. Before he could question her, she dropped her hand to squeeze the hard length of his cock. "I'm much more interested in this kind of hard."

Christ, he was going to need to tie her down. Those wandering hands of hers would be the end of him otherwise.

"Bedroom's third door on the right."

"Now we're talking."

She spun away from him and started walking the length of the hall. He didn't move, preferring to watch her. She paused just outside his bedroom door, lifting her hands up to her neck and unhooking her dress. She winked and disappeared through the doorway as the fabric fell.

Finley used the moment of solitude to suck in a sharp breath.

Fuck, what was he doing? This was too fast. Too soon. He never slept with a woman he'd just met. But this wasn't some random woman. It was the one in all the realms made solely for him.

*Quinn.*

His purpose.

His everything.

He had to have her, ruin her for all others. Make sure she knew that from this moment on, he was it for her. That she'd never need or want another. That by the time he was done with her, she wouldn't even remember anyone else.

He was hers, and she was his. All that was left was to claim her.

With only that thought in his mind, Finley took off down the hall, tugging off his tie and jacket, leaving them forgotten in the hall-way. His shirt was halfway unbuttoned by the time he got to the door.

The sight that greeted him nearly sent him to his knees.

She'd removed her dress and stood facing him wearing only her elbow-length gloves, sky-high heels, and a smile.

"Fuck."

"Took you long enough. I was about to get started without you." She smirked and crooked her finger. "Come here, lover boy."

"No."

"No?"

"On your knees."

A flush of arousal swept down her skin, tightening the rosy bud of her nipples into stiff peaks. She might like to boss him around, but she liked it more when he did it. Which was perfect because so did he.

Lip caught between her teeth, she slowly dropped to her knees, eyes locked on his. "What now?"

"Arms clasped behind you."

Once again, she was quick to obey, and the move pulled her shoulders back and pushed her breasts forward.

She was a fucking wet dream kneeling there, awaiting his next command. It was going to be hell trying not to rush through this.

He moved forward, unbuttoning the rest of his shirt, taking the time to fold it and set it neatly on his dresser while she watched him with desire-glazed eyes. Then he reached for his belt and had to swallow back a groan when she pressed her thighs together to try to hide what watching him undress was doing to her.

He rolled up the belt and set it on top of his shirt. Then he smoothed his hand over her head, grabbing the length of her braid and tugging her head back so her eyes met his.

"I want to see those ruby lips wrapped around my cock."

She moaned, her arms lifting. He gave her hair a light tug.

"No hands. Not yet."

"But how am I—"

"Use your mouth."

Her full body flush deepened. Leaning forward on her knees, she took his zipper between her teeth, stealing just a second to rub her cheek against his erection. It was a mild act of disobedience, but since it caused his cock to swell and balls to tighten, he wasn't going to complain. This time.

Once his zipper was down, she used her nose to spread the gaping fabric wider and then sought out his heavy length. Her hot breaths and wet heat were the sweetest torture. When she sucked the tip of him in her mouth, his head fell back and his hand fisted in her hair.

"Fuck, yes, princess. Just like that. Show me how much you can take."

She made a humming sound around him, tipping her chin up just a bit so she could hold his gaze as she started to slide down his throbbing shaft.

"That's it. That's my good girl."

Her eyes fluttered at the praise right as he bottomed out against the back of her throat.

"Can you hold me here?"

She hummed again, her throat fluttering obscenely around his thick shaft. Her eyes were jewel-bright, not quite with tears, but she was definitely working hard to breathe with him filling her.

He started to pull back, chuckling softly when she followed him.

"It's okay, sweetheart. We'll save that for another time. You can use your hands. One on me, one on yourself. But don't come. That's for me."

The silk length of her glove was the perfect accompaniment to the damp heat of her mouth. She was enjoying the slide of fabric against her clit too, if her wanton moans were any indication. As she worked him, her lipstick left little rings around him, marking the places she'd been. He felt the need to mark her body in a similar fashion. A carnal expedition where he was the conqueror and her body the foreign land.

It wasn't long before an orgasm was building in the base of his spine, but he wouldn't let himself come yet. Not until she did.

"Enough."

She sat back on her heels, her chest rising and falling with each shuddering breath.

"Can you make it to the bed on your own?"

"Yes, sir." She peeked up at him through her lashes. "Or should I call you Daddy?"

His chest hollowed out, and beads of precum leaked out of him. He'd never had a preference for such things but hearing her call him Daddy in that sultry voice did all sorts of things to him. He knew he'd be hearing the echo in his head long after the night was over.

He crouched down so their faces were level. "Is that what you want, princess?"

"Yes, Daddy."

His eyes searched hers, looking for any sign of hesitation. But there was none. Only desire . . . and devotion.

"Then be Daddy's good girl and get on the bed."

She rushed to obey.

When she leaned over to climb up, he caught sight of the arousal sliding down her thighs and her swollen lower lips. He stopped her with a hand on her back.

"Stay right there."

He knelt behind her, following the path of her arousal with his tongue all the way up to her beautiful pink cunt. His hand drifted over her back, grasping the full globe of her ass and squeezing hard as he spread her wide.

She moaned, pushing her hips back into his face. He ate her like a starving man who'd just been given his favorite meal. It wasn't long before she was writhing against him, chanting his name.

"Fin, please. God, I want to come."

"Not yet. I want to be inside you when you fall apart."

"Then do it, I can't—"

He pulled away, spanking her pussy hard and fast, cutting off her words. "You can and will. Get on your back."

She cried out, but it was a sound of pure pleasure. It wouldn't take much to send her over the edge, but she would bloody well wait until he gave her permission.

Her legs were trembling so badly, he had to grasp her by the waist and lift her up onto the mattress. She crawled to the center of the bed and then laid down on her back. He climbed up after, straddling her thighs.

She gave him a confused frown when he leaned forward, but not to claim her lips. Instead, he turned his head to the side and took the edge of her glove in his mouth, kissing and licking the skin just above and below it before taking the scrap of fabric in his teeth and peeling it down her arm. Arm bared, he sat back and let the glove fall in a pool of silk on her belly before doing the same to her other one. Task finished, he picked them both up and got off the bed.

"Where are you going?"

"I'm not going anywhere, princess. Neither are you. Arms above your head."

Her pulse fluttered rapidly in her neck, but she did as he'd asked.

"Good girl," he said, trailing the tips of his fingers along the underside of her arm. When he got to her wrists, he tied first one then the other to the headboard, using her gloves as restraints.

"Are you comfortable?"

All she could manage was a nod.

"If that changes, you need to let me know, all right, princess?"

"Y-yes, Daddy."

He leaned down and kissed her hard. "I'm going to fuck you now. You can come whenever you want, but you'll say my name when you do it. Understand?"

"Yes. Yes. Yes."

She was completely lost to her pleasure, her pupils blown wide, purple eyes hazy. He'd never seen anything so beautiful in his entire life.

He almost regretted not drawing the moment out longer, making her come time and again before finally sliding into her, but he couldn't. He needed to be inside of her, to make her his. There would be time for that later. They had nothing but time.

"Look at me, Quinn."

Her eyes found his as he lined himself up at her entrance. She was so wet he slid in easily, filling her in one deep thrust and making them both moan at the pleasure of it. Her inner muscles clamped around him, holding him tighter than any fist.

"God, Quinn. You feel so fucking good."

"You too. So good."

He pulled out only to slam back in.

"Fin, please. I'm so close."

He continued to thrust, hard and deep, combining it with the rough swipe of his thumb over her swollen clit. It wasn't long before she was bucking beneath him.

"Oh! Fuck, yes, Finley!" Her back arched, her arms straining against their bindings as she came.

"Jesus," he grunted, her pussy like a fucking vise as it milked him, begging him to join her. His body was helpless to resist the silent command, and a handful of frantic thrusts later, he was right there with her, pumping rope after rope of his cum inside her. Where it belonged.

He leaned down, claiming her lips in a fierce but tender kiss, not ready to pull out of her yet.

"I . . . that was amazing," she panted.

He couldn't help his smug grin. "I told you I had a plan. Just wait until you see what I have in store for part two."

"I . . ." she chuckled. "Fuck, I can hardly talk. Bravo, sir."

"Daddy," he growled in her ear.

She shivered. "Can I touch you now? Please . . . Daddy."

Finley leaned up, freeing both her wrists. She curled into him immediately, running her hands up and down his chest, nuzzling into his neck and making soft sounds of contentment.

Heart still thundering, he wrapped his arms tightly around her, holding her close. Pressing his lips to her forehead, he whispered, "You're mine now. My good girl. I'm never letting you go."

She stiffened and blew out a breath. "It's a pity you had to go and be so perfect."

The happy buzz he'd been floating in vanished, and his muscles tensed. "What do you mean?"

She cupped his cheek in her hand and tilted his face until he was staring into two pools of rippling burgundy. "Because you made me want to keep you, and I can't." She sighed heavily, the sound filled with regret. "In fact, I better do this right now, or I'm going to lose my nerve."

He jerked, trying to sit upright, but she rolled on top of him.

"For what it's worth, I'm sorry. I really wish things were different." Then she leaned down and kissed him one last time. When she pulled away, she stared deep into his eyes, whispering, "Tonight never happened. You and I never met."

# CHAPTER SIXTEEN
## FINLEY

Finley gasped like a drowning man coming up for air. The pressure in his chest was excruciating, like he hadn't drawn a full breath in hours instead of seconds. His heart ached, the poor muscle feeling bruised and battered, as if someone had been using it as a football for the better part of a season.

He groaned, his head swimming.

"Do you have any idea what you've done, Satori?" he rasped, his voice hoarse with disuse.

When she didn't immediately respond, he realized something was different. He tried to sit, but tubes of various lengths and sizes jutted out from both of his arms. He blinked, finally giving his surroundings a thorough inspection.

Why was he in a hospital bed? No, this wasn't a hospital. He was in the medical wing of the Brotherhood's main office.

He tried to sit up, but his body didn't seem to want to obey him.

The door crashed open. "Finley, thank God."

"Nate?" he croaked. "What's happened?"

The only explanation he could come up with was that something had gone horribly wrong while they were conducting their investigation.

"I could ask you the same bloody thing," he said, his voice tight with worry.

"Where's Quinn?"

Nate walked around the end of his bed, moving over to his left to pull back a light blue curtain.

Finley's ravaged heart seized when he saw what laid beyond the pale fabric. Quinn was lying on the bed, unconscious.

The body that wouldn't respond moments prior knifed upright, tubes yanking free of their moorings as he surged upward off the bed, intent on reaching her.

"Finley, wait . . . shit." Nate leapt to his side, catching him as Finley's knees gave out. "Take it easy, will you?"

"What's . . . wrong with me?" he panted. The small rush of adrenaline had wiped him of his energy. He was completely spent.

"You were cursed."

"Cursed?"

"Blimey, Fin. Don't you remember anything?"

Finley lifted a hand to his head as Nate helped him sit back down. "Pieces. Everything is all jumbled. Mostly I remember coming to see you and . . . Quinn."

Why did her name send a pang of absolute agony through him?

When the answer came to him, so did the feelings of heartbreak and betrayal.

She'd robbed him of everything.

Nate sent a worried glance in her direction. "Why is she still under?"

"Pardon?"

"Why didn't both of you come back? You went under at the same time. I assumed you'd come back together."

Finley's temples throbbed, the words coming out of Nate's mouth not making a bit of sense.

"Nate, what the bloody hell are you talking about?"

"Fin, mate, what's the last thing you remember?"

"Before waking up here?"

"Sure."

He had no intention of telling Nate what Quinn had done. How he'd found his purpose only for her to tear away the moment of knowing and so carelessly extract a vital piece of his soul in the process.

All this time . . . they could have been together all this time. The possibility of who and what she was to him had been bad enough when Nate brought it up, but to learn the truth—that his soul *had* recognized her, had known right away that he was hers, and she'd been the one to make him forget . . . it was unforgivable. A betrayal of the highest order.

He wanted to believe that she didn't understand what she'd done. How the magic only worked once. If she hadn't given the memory back, he would have spent the rest of his immortal life never knowing the missing piece of his soul was right there within reach.

As it was, he'd been mourning a woman he hadn't even remembered existed for the last two years. No wonder he hadn't wanted anyone else. The part of him that knew she was out there had been yearning for her all this time. No one else would do.

How could anyone ever live up when you'd already found your soulmate?

Quinn had stripped away the truth, but a Guardian's magic still ran through his veins. The moment of knowing—that lightning bolt to the heart that screamed she was the one—only happened once. But part of him had known, had been drawn to her, even if all this time he hadn't understood why.

Sure, he had it back now. The memory, the knowing, answers to questions he hadn't even known to ask. But at what cost?

What could ever really exist between them now that he knew what she'd done? Now that he knew how little she must have cared to have kept it from him all this time.

Jesus.

Two. Fucking. Years.

"It's all right, mate. Just take your time," Nate said, placing a hand on the back of his shoulder.

"Sorry, my head's all muddled. I remember searching for Marquez, but not much after that."

Nate frowned. "Tomas Marquez?"

"Yeah."

"Fin, you were at his funeral. He died six months ago."

"What?"

Nate gave him a searching look. "Maybe I should call a healer in here. Get you properly checked out."

Finley curled a fist in Nate's suit jacket, holding him in place. "Why don't you tell me what *you* remember."

It wasn't a suggestion.

"I mean, there's not much to tell. I asked you and Quinn to stop in to check out a cursed object that came into our possession. Actually, if I'm being candid, it was sent here but addressed to you."

"You're just telling me this now?"

"I didn't know who to trust. There were markings on it indicating it was tied to the Mobius Council. I wanted to see how Quinn reacted."

*You wanted to see if she was involved.*

A scathing admonition was on the tip of his tongue, but Nate's explanation left him conflicted. On one hand, he didn't appreciate the Guardian trying to trick Quinn into revealing things without being forthcoming himself. On the other . . . Quinn was hardly a pillar of virtue, as she'd so recently shown. He couldn't exactly blame the man for keeping his cards close to his chest until he knew where she stood. And it wasn't as easy to jump to her defense when he knew how far she'd go to protect her own interests.

His stomach tightened as something oily and slick churned inside it. Now that he knew what she'd done, how could he ever trust her or her motives again?

"You think she sent it?" he finally asked, voice flat.

"The thought had crossed my mind, but I didn't really believe she was behind it. I was more interested in finding out if she recognized it, or better yet, if she knew who created it."

Hearing that Nate thought she was innocent made him feel marginally better. At least he wasn't a complete fool for hoping the same.

"So the whole Tomas thing . . ."

"Must have been a side effect of the curse."

Finley rubbed his aching head. "It all felt so real."

"All we've been able to discern about the object is that it's triggered by touch and that the curse was telepathic in nature."

"Was?"

"The object became inert after the curse took hold."

Finley scrubbed a hand over his chin. "And it was addressed to me?"

Nate gave him a wary nod. "Whoever sent it intended for you to remain lost in your own mind."

There was one ex-member of Mobius he had no doubt wanted him out of the picture. Mikel could have set it up for that package to arrive weeks ago. If Nate had reached out sooner, or if they hadn't been in Novasgard, there's no telling how differently things might have played out. Not just for him personally, but for all of them.

*Christ, what a bloody mess.*

Finley frowned, something Nate said not sitting quite right. "If it was my mind I was lost in, why was Quinn in there with me?"

"No idea. You sure you didn't just imagine her? Wishful thinking, perhaps?"

He considered the possibility but immediately dismissed it. There was no way he'd ever have recovered those missing memories if she hadn't been there to return them. Her magic was the equivalent of a scalpel, and when wielded, it essentially allowed her to surgically remove whatever she wanted. There wasn't a trace of what she'd taken in his subconscious for him to remember on his own.

"We were definitely together."

"Hmm . . ." Nate looked away, clearly thinking hard. "Maybe it was some other mental plane created from pieces of both your minds since you both activated the curse? Or maybe the curse was tied to your telepathic gifts, forging a link between you? There's no way to know, really. But one thing's certain, Quinn is still trapped there."

"Why her and not me?"

Nate shrugged. "I was hoping you'd be able to tell me that. I do feel a little responsible for her. After all, it's my fault she touched the card before I could explain what it was."

"The card?"

"It was the object bearing the curse. Do you remember that small rectangular card I had on my desk? The black one with the sigil?"

Finley nodded, the description calling to mind a hazy recollection. "Why didn't you warn us about it?"

Nate gave a sheepish shrug. "I wanted to get her honest reaction. When she seemed to recognize it, I thought for sure we'd get some answers, but then you both went and touched it, and well . . . here we are."

"Bugger."

"That about sums it up."

Christ, if everything after touching the card was a result of the curse, then hardly anything of their time at headquarters had been real. Not even Nate's revelations about Quinn. It had all been in his mind.

But if it was the case, how had he stumbled upon the truth of Quinn being his purpose when she'd removed the memory? Had his subconscious pieced it together, recognizing the signs even when the rest of his brain could not? Or was it being telepathically connected to Quinn that made the difference and allowed him to finally see what had been staring him in the face?

It was . . . a lot to process. More than he could handle right now.

Finley tried to sort through his tangled mess of thoughts, to organize them in a way that would explain everything. When that failed, he settled on trying to figure out how he'd managed to break free while she was still trapped inside.

"She kept saying something about saving me. About how I needed to remember what was real in order to see through the deception."

Nate made a considering noise. "Sounds like maybe she's the one that helped you break free."

The sting of her betrayal was still so fresh, but even so, the idea that she'd been wholly focused on rescuing him, even at the risk of having to out herself in the process, softened some of the ache. She'd done that for him, even knowing what it might cost her in the end. It couldn't have been an easy choice. Not unless she cared about him more than she did about herself.

"The entire time we were together, she was focused on helping me escape."

His head snapped up, and he stared at Nate with wide eyes. His shock at his sudden realization only just eclipsed the shooting pain the action sent crashing through his skull.

"Quinn didn't know she was also under the effects of the spell. It tricked her, the same as me, but instead of scrambling her memories, it made her believe I was the only one in trouble. The curse got its hooks far deeper in her than they were in me because Quinn never knew enough to try and fight it off. Christ, Nate. These kinds of spells ramp up exponentially. The longer she's under the effects of it, the less likely we're going to be able to save her."

Nate paled. "Well then, it seems like you need to go in and help her like she did for you."

Finley nodded, having already come to the same conclusion. Quinn may have broken his heart with her thoughtless actions, but he still loved her. He would never leave her to face this on her own. She'd tried to keep it from him, but it was still his duty—his right— to protect her. If the Brotherhood was to be believed, it's what he'd been born for.

He tugged the tubes free and stood, pleased that he only swayed a little once he was upright.

"Are you up for this?" Nate asked.

"Yes."

His friend gave him a knowing look. "Would you admit it if you weren't?"

"Not a fucking chance."

Nate sighed.

Finley moved over to Quinn, his throat tight. He'd been avoiding looking at her until now. The sight of her lying unconscious was far too painful to process. He took her hand, hating how fragile it appeared dwarfed by his.

"Did you know?" he asked, his voice low.

"Know what?"

"That she was mine?"

Nate clapped him on the shoulder. "Mate, everybody knew."

Finley let out a humorless laugh. "And no one thought to let me in on the secret?"

"What secret? A Guardian always knows when they've found the one, it's in our blood. We just assumed you were playing some kind of game."

Finley finally allowed himself to look at Quinn's face, his heart spasming painfully. "One of us was."

Nate sucked in a breath. "Finley, I—"

"Leave it. It doesn't matter now. Will you give us some privacy?"

Nate gestured to the door. "I'll be just outside. I'll check in every hour to make sure you're both all right."

Finley nodded, not paying attention as his friend left the room. Still cradling Quinn's hand in his, he sat down on the bed beside her, using his other hand to brush a few stray stands of hair off her forehead.

"When this is all over, Satori, you and I are going to have a very serious talk. You have some explaining to do, and I have some decisions to make."

# CHAPTER SEVENTEEN
## QUINN

"Finley . . . Finley, wait! Where are you going? Are you really just going to leave me here?"

Quinn's heart shattered as the man she loved, the man she'd sacrificed everything for, turned on his heel and walked away, abandoning her without a word.

She dropped to her knees, great heaving sobs ripping her apart as she curled in on herself.

Alone.

She'd always been destined to be alone.

She knew better. Had seen what happened when someone was stupid enough to give a piece of themselves to someone else for safe keeping. How it destroyed them when the other person inevitably left. Willingly or not.

She was supposed to be smarter than that. Hell, she'd spent her entire life trying to prevent this exact moment from ever playing out. She vowed never to put herself in a position to be broken the way her mom had. It's why she'd taken Finley's memory in the first place. If he didn't remember her, he couldn't go looking for her, she wouldn't become more attached, and their enemies couldn't use their relationship against them.

But it hadn't been that simple.

Nothing about her relationship with Finley ever was. Not two years ago and certainly not now that she'd gotten to know the incredible man beneath the smoldering good looks.

It had taken every single part of her to maintain the pretense that they didn't have a past. That she didn't know exactly what it would be like if she surrendered to the connection that had always existed between them. She'd gotten so used to denying anything had ever happened between them that she'd started to believe her own story. At least, until the moon rose and she'd lie alone in her bed with only her memory of their single night together to keep her company.

Just one night had been enough to ensure she'd never get over him. Never get him out of her system. She'd thought about him every day for months, and then, just when she believed she'd managed to do the impossible, he popped up again. This time attached to Lina.

There'd been no avoiding him then, though Lord knows she tried. She'd done everything she could think of to keep him at arm's length. But even as she'd been trying to keep him away, part of her wanted more. It wanted the man who'd slow danced with her in a dimly lit alcove. Who'd taken control of her pleasure in a way no one before or since had ever dared. She wanted the man who'd claimed her heart with a single, searing look.

That's all it had taken. A single look.

He'd walked into the room and her lungs stopped. She hadn't understood her reaction; it had never been like that before. Immediate. All-consuming. Naively, she hadn't questioned it. Instead, she chalked it up to just another night, just another man. One she'd leave behind come the morning, same as she always did.

She'd been lying to herself about her feelings for him from the start, but they were never supposed to have more than one night.

She was never supposed to go and fall in love.

Throat raw, eyes swollen, and face wet with tears, Quinn picked herself up off the floor. She was too consumed by her grief to do more than note the fire crackling in the hearth and the snow falling heavily outside the floor-to-ceiling windows. But as she walked deeper into the room, the ache in her heart hardened and then transformed.

With each step, she was waking up, and then suddenly, Quinn wasn't sad at all.

She was fucking livid.

After everything she'd done to save him, that asshole had the audacity to ditch her at his penthouse and take off without so much as a thank-you? She'd even settle for a passionate fuck-you-very-much. Anything other than blatant disregard.

As if she was nothing.

As if what existed between them was nothing.

Needing an outlet for her anger, she screamed and swung her arm out, knocking over each precious item Finley so carefully displayed on the mantel. She didn't even flinch at the resounding crash as they hit the floor.

She hoped they were priceless and irreplaceable.

Spotting a few unshattered pieces, she stomped on them for good measure. When a metal dish simply rolled away, she tore off her stiletto, dropped down, and tried to crack it open with the heel. Needless to say, her weapon of choice wasn't very effective. Realizing she hadn't so much as made a dent, she flung the seven-hundred-dollar shoe toward the window with a furious growl. Then she took off its partner and chucked it behind her without looking.

It never hit the ground.

"Having a bit of a meltdown, Satori?"

Her back stiffened.

*Oh, now he decides to show up. Of fucking course.*

She turned slowly, chest still heaving as she spotted Finley standing beside one of the armchairs, one hand in his pocket, the other holding her shoe.

"Drop this?" he asked neutrally.

She scowled at him. "You don't just get to waltz in here and act like everything's normal."

He tossed her stiletto over his shoulder. "Oh good, I wasn't relishing the idea of having to pretend that I wasn't pissed with you either."

"Pissed with me? You're the one who just"—she flung her arm out dramatically—"walked off into the sunset. You didn't even stick around to fight for us before you assumed the worst and abandoned me."

His brows pulled together as he gave her an incredulous stare. "After what you did, do you really think you have the right to lecture me on my behavior?"

"After the promises you made me, yeah, I think I do," she shot back, crossing her arms beneath her chest.

"Newsflash, princess, you do not have the moral high ground here."

Since when had that ever stopped her?

She stomped forward, significantly shorter than usual without the aid of her heels. "Well then, welcome to the mosh pit, Batman, because *newsflash,* you don't have it either."

"What is it that you think I've done exactly?"

"You. Left. Me." Each word was bit off and punctuated by the press of her finger into his chest. "Again."

"What the hell are you talking about? When have I ever left you? If anything, I'm here to hunt you down."

"YOU ALWAYS LEAVE!"

Quinn didn't know where the enraged scream came from. It didn't even sound like her as the words flew from her lips. Spinning away, she shoved her fingers in her hair, blinking rapidly as she tried to make sense of things. This wasn't her. She didn't get into screaming matches—and she definitely didn't let someone know when they'd hurt her. She buried that shit deep. And if a comeback was required, she eviscerated whoever dared to cross her with a well-aimed verbal blow. Generally speaking, the more pissed she was, the colder her voice got, never . . . whatever the hell that was.

Where had it even come from?

Head aching, Quinn had to squeeze her eyes shut tight against a small explosion of lights behind her eyelids. When she opened them again, she took in the penthouse with a frown.

*When did I get here?* How *did I get here?*

Finley grasped her arm and hauled her back to face him. "Oh no, you don't get to make a baseless accusation like that and then just walk away. Explain yourself. When did I leave you?"

"F-Fin?"

"I'm waiting for your answer, princess."

She narrowed her eyes, trying to remember his question, but as she stared at him, the living room began to flicker. Between one blink and the next, she went from standing before Finley in the living room to kneeling beside his lifeless body in the vineyard.

"No. Oh no, not again."

*He will never be yours.*

Quinn jerked away from the voice slithering through her mind. It didn't sound like her voice at all. In fact, it sounded like . . . Mikel.

*There is no future that exists where he doesn't end up just like this.*

"No," she moaned. "He's alive. Finley's alive. I . . . I saved him."

*But for how long? How many times have you watched him nearly die to protect you? How many more must you endure before he stops courting death?*

Quinn flinched at the reminder of all the times Finley had gotten hurt because of her. She turned away from his still form, but no matter where her eyes landed, his body and the swirling pool of his blood were right there taunting her.

*You will give him your heart, only to see it torn apart.*

She shuddered, wanting to deny the words but unable to. After all, Mikel was only giving voice to her deepest fears. He wasn't saying a single thing she hadn't thought at least once herself.

*Loving him will destroy you.*

"Quinn. Quinn!" Finley's voice, low and urgent, like he'd been trying to get her attention for a while, finally reached her. "Sweetheart, you have to fight it. It's not real. None of what you're seeing right now is real. Come back. Come back to me."

She blinked, and there was a moment of disorientation as the world tipped and spun. When she opened her eyes, she was standing in the penthouse once more. Chest heavy. Heart bruised. Hope shattered.

Because Mikel may not have been real, but what he'd said about Finley had been right.

Loving her would be the death of him. And if—when—she lost him, it would be the end of her too.

Finley wasn't the kind of man she would survive. Already he'd snuck in and laid claim. Made her vulnerable. Weak. She'd managed to safeguard her heart for decades behind walls so thick no one ever came close to breaching them.

No one until him.

And he hadn't just swooped in like a caped crusader; he'd robbed her like a thief in the night. Stealing her heart before she even realized it was missing. Capturing it like it had been his all along. Like it had never really belonged to her at all. Like she'd always been keeping it safe . . . for him.

And that was the problem, wasn't it?

Because no one could live without their heart, and Finley was hers.

There was a sharp crack, and then pain blossomed across her cheek as her head snapped to the side.

"Ouch!"

Finley stepped close, cradling her face in his palms and holding her still as his eyes searched hers. "I'm sorry. I was losing you again. I didn't know what else to do, and I couldn't let you fall back under the spell."

She pulled out of his hold, rubbing a hand over her smarting cheek. "Spell? Finley, what are you talking about? Have you been drinking? You're not making any sense."

"No, dammit. Listen to me. You've been cursed." He grabbed her biceps and gave her a slight shake.

Something about the word tickled the back of her mind. "No . . ." she said slowly, remembering. "You were the one who was cursed."

"Not just me, love. We were both trapped in some sort of joint mind prison, but you helped me break free."

His words sounded familiar, but when she couldn't immediately recall the details, she panicked. Quinn had never forgotten a thing a day in her life, so either he was lying to her, or something was seriously wrong. Given the dazed, slightly hazy quality of her thoughts, she was going to err in his favor. Finley was a lot of things, but he wasn't a liar.

"So then why are you here?"

"Because I came back to get you."

"But I was the one saving you."

He let out a frustrated growl. "I don't know how you put up with me when I was like this. You must have the patience of a fucking saint."

"It's one of the few perks of having to put up with you for the last several months. I'm awaiting the announcement of my canonization any day now."

"Clearly, I spoke too soon."

They stared at each other for a long moment before sharing a smile.

"Why is it I feel most like myself when I'm taking shots at you?" she asked.

Finley chuckled, shaking his head. "I couldn't say. Bickering must be our love language."

Quinn snorted. "I thought it was our version of foreplay."

"That too," he conceded.

Their smiles stretched, though Finley's soon faded.

"I know things are far from perfect between us right now. And I'd be lying if I said I wasn't absolutely furious with you. But Quinn, darling, I need you to snap out of this. It's not safe for you to stay here."

Her chest cracked in two, not because of what he said, but the tender way he said it. She wished she knew why he was mad at her so she could apologize and fix it. All she wanted was to curl up in his arms.

All she wanted was him.

Finley ran his thumb over the crests of her cheeks, and she soaked in the gentle contact, wrapping her hands around his, holding him there. He repeated the motion, but instead of soothing her, it caused her head to throb.

Everything felt . . . wrong. Twisted. Like she'd stepped through a funhouse mirror and was living on the other side. Panic gripped her, even as another part of her subconscious crooned that everything was fine. She was safe. Home.

The contradicting sensations brought her a jolt of clarity, but the brief flicker wasn't enough to steady her, and she was soon floating in the haze once more. The harder she tried to cling to a thought, the faster it unraveled.

She couldn't remember why they were here. Why she'd been so angry. Or why looking at Finley made her heart splinter.

"It's happening again. I can see it in your eyes. Please, princess. Fight it. Stay here with me. Better yet, come home to me."

She wanted to. God did she ever. The only thing that felt remotely stable right now was him.

"My mind is . . . drifting. Everything feels so jumbled. I find something to hold on to, only to have it blow away again. Things I knew . . . the things I did . . . I'm losing them."

His hands spasmed beneath hers, his eyes flashing with panic. "That's the curse."

"What do you mean?"

"It shatters your mind by taking away the things that make you whole. It starts small, siphoning off little things you won't miss. And once those are gone, it takes bigger pieces, draining them so fast all you can do is watch them swirl away."

"It's stealing my memories."

"Not just memories. Fundamental truths. *Your* truths. It reshapes events in your life, twisting the outcome until you are unmade. The only way to fight back is to find and own your truth."

"How do you know that?"

"Because that's what you did for me."

"I did?"

"You did, princess."

"How?"

"You helped me find something I didn't know I lost."

"What was it?"

"My purpose."

"I don't think I have a purpose."

"Maybe you call it something else?"

Quinn frowned, none of that sounding familiar. She slipped out of his hold, wandering closer to the windows and the falling snow. Her mind blanked and when she jerked back to attention, she had no idea how much time she'd just lost. Seconds? Minutes? An hour?

It couldn't be long now. The pieces of her were already starting to fall away.

Finley was still there, studying her reflection in the glass. Coming to stand by her side, he asked, "Do you remember what you shouted at me earlier?"

Quinn rubbed at her temple, trying to bring back the words. "No. I'm sorry."

"You were angry at me for leaving. You said I always leave."

The words tumbled around in her mind before igniting a spark of recognition. "Everybody leaves."

He didn't touch her, but his gaze was laser-focused on hers in the windowpane. "Who left you, princess?"

"My father. Lina. Alistair. Sylvia. *You.*"

He was quiet for a long moment, his brows low over sparkling hazel eyes. "You mean they died."

"Can you think of a more permanent way of leaving someone?"

"I didn't die, princess. I'm right here."

"Yes, you did. I watched you. Twice. First in the . . ." She struggled to hold on to the image, but this one was burned deep, and it couldn't be taken from her easily. "Vineyard. And then again today."

He turned to face her. "So that's what this is about. You're scared you're going to lose me."

"You're not a toy I'm going to leave in the yard."

"Quinn, I would never leave you intentionally. Not unless you asked me to go."

"You left me today. You got mad, and you left."

"That's not what happened."

"Yes, it is."

He must have been tired of talking to her profile because he took her chin in his hand and turned it until she was forced to meet his gaze. "No, sweetheart. It isn't. I have never, not once, willingly left you. If we're being honest, I'm pretty sure I've spent the last several years of my life just trying to get back to you."

She wasn't sure why, but his admission had her on the verge of tears. "But the vineyard—"

"Was out of my control."

Her throat constricted. "I can't . . . feel the things I feel for you if I'm just going to have my heart broken. I won't. I won't let you hurt me."

"What is it you feel for me, Satori?"

Quinn pressed her lips together and shook her head.

He leaned down, his lips resting at her ear. "Tell me."

"No."

Finley sighed. "I should have known you'd be stubborn right up to the last."

Her lips twitched, but she remained silent.

"You told me a story once. About the kind of man you wanted to give your heart to. Do you remember?"

Quinn frowned as an image bloomed in her mind of a strong man with twinkling eyes holding a dark-haired woman in his arms, dancing with her. Her heart filled with a painful yearning, but the picture snuffed out, leaving her without an answer to his question.

"I . . . no, I don't."

"It's okay, because I do."

Fin waved a hand, and the window between them and the snow vanished. Quinn braced herself, expecting the wind to pull her to the cement several stories below, but when she released her breath, she realized they were no longer standing in a penthouse. They were in the middle of a glittering wonderland. Stars filled the moonlit sky above as snow gently fell, blanketing the world around them.

"Dance with me, Satori."

"What? Here?"

"Here. For the rest of our lives. Take your pick."

Quinn swallowed, not sure why a dance would make her feel this way. Lightheaded, shaky, filled with hope.

She accepted his hand, and he grinned. The look shot a bolt of heat through her, and she blushed. She didn't even know this man's name, and he was making her feel . . . things. It shouldn't be possible for a stranger to make her feel this way.

She peeked up at him from the corner of her eye, trying to memorize the chiseled set of his jaw and the way his eyelashes left shadows on his cheeks. He was so beautiful. She thought she could probably stare at him all night and never tire of it.

Then he led her out to the center of the courtyard, spinning her away from him before reeling her back in. She laughed when she crashed into his body, his warm chuckles joining hers and soon filling the night around them.

And when he took her in his arms and started humming some horribly off-key song in her ear, she snuggled closer, thinking that the smell of clove and mint was her favorite as they swayed to a nonexistent beat. But when she pulled back to look up at the man holding her so tenderly, that was when she *knew*.

She may not have known anything else in that moment. Not the day. Not this place. Not his name—or hers for that matter. But this she knew, without a doubt.

It was her one fundamental truth.

"I love you."

# CHAPTER EIGHTEEN
## QUINN

Waking up in a glorified hospital bed had been a shock, to say the least. But not more of one than the reserved and almost detached way Finley had been treating her since he'd helped her break free of her cursed sleep.

Apparently, all the fairy tales spouting how curses were broken when the prince gave his princess true love's kiss had been a bunch of glossed-over bullshit. Quinn found it oddly appropriate that the real-life version required more of a sacrifice in order for the couple to earn their happy ending. In reality, the curse was only broken once the princess got out of her own way and openly expressed both her fears and her feelings to the prince. Like a grownup who was worthy of a healthy, loving, adult relationship. Either way, this was supposed to be the part of the story that picked up after 'and they both lived happily ever after.'

Or that's what she'd assumed would be the case after the curse was broken. In her version, the prince stood halfway across the room, staring at her with an unreadable expression instead of kissing her senseless and proclaiming his undying love.

And this was the reason Quinn had never much liked fairy tales. They were oversimplified children's stories filled with misogynistic lies. Even after defeating a dragon, the prince and princess couldn't seem to get their shit together.

Thinking perhaps it was simply concern for her wellbeing keeping him away, she'd hoped he would snap out of his strange mood once the healer gave Quinn the all clear.

No such luck.

Nate had been waiting on the sidelines, ushering them both into his office for a full debrief as soon as they'd thrown on their freshly laundered clothes—though Quinn's panties were notably missing. She assumed they were still in Finley's pocket, but his frosty countenance kept her from confirming it.

That sexy little showdown of theirs, at least, had been real. It was everything else beginning the moment Nate sat at his desk that was suspect. Quinn supposed there was an argument to be made that since their minds had been interacting with one another the entire time, the conversations and confessions they'd shared while trapped were just as real as anything else.

Listening to Nate and Finley fill her in about the details of the spell had been enlightening once her initial disbelief had passed. She still couldn't wrap her head around how Mikel had managed to lay such an effective, albeit simple, trap. Sending it to Fin via the Brotherhood had been a stroke of genius. Finley wouldn't question an item brought to his attention by them the same way he would something sent anonymously to his house. And Mikel couldn't have possibly known it, but them not being alerted to its existence until after his death practically ensured that their guards would be down.

Then again, he hadn't been the type to care about *when* his brand of justice was delivered. Only that it was, that it hurt, and that it would scar.

Yes, the whole thing reeked of Mikel, and she knew it was all her fault.

Even though the package bore Finley's name, Quinn was under

no illusions about the intended recipient of that particular gift. Watching her suffer as the man she loved unraveled right in front of her . . . that was the end goal. Finley had simply been collateral damage, shattering his mind the means of her torture. But it had never been about him. Only getting back at her.

Quinn was willing to bet Mikel had sent his creation within hours of learning about her deception. That the curse was payback for the fake Codex. She'd denied him what he wanted, so he'd reacted in kind by going after her Guardian.

Just like he'd promised.

That vile and manipulative sack of shit would have been absolutely beside himself with glee when he'd found out Quinn had also fallen victim to his little surprise. He would have seen it as his good fortune paying dividends as always. He was absolutely the type of man to be pragmatic about her downfall. If he couldn't bring her to heel, he might as well remove her from the board entirely.

That was her working theory, anyway. With the bastard reduced to little more than rotting bits, she couldn't exactly ask him. But she knew firsthand just how depraved Mikel Drake's mind had been. She could piece together the truth.

In the aftermath of the revelations and what they'd been through, Quinn was feeling raw and a little untethered. Finley knew the truth about what she'd done, about how she felt, and he hadn't said a word about it. He'd barely spoken to her at all beyond unavoidable chatter. It was as if he was trying to remain just polite enough that she couldn't find fault with him. But if that was the case, he clearly didn't know her as well as he thought he did because she could find fault with anything.

Especially being ignored, or worse, iced out.

Which is exactly what this closed-off version of Finley felt like. He was holding himself back, keeping his thoughts and emotions to himself. If he was pissed, she'd much prefer it if he would rail at her because then at least she'd know what he was thinking. But this silence was absolute torture. She'd never felt farther away from him in her life.

He was paying more attention to strangers on the street than he was to her right now. Oh, she knew he was aware of her. Even staring out the window of the cab driving them back to his penthouse, his body was angled toward hers, mirroring her position. But his mind was a thousand miles away.

She risked a glance at him, hating the distance stretching between them with every mile. There was nothing more intimate than walking through someone's subconscious. She should feel closer to him than ever. Instead, he was pushing her away.

What she didn't understand was why.

Okay, so maybe she had an idea, but she'd thought those things had been settled and that his coming back to save her was a sign she'd been forgiven. Maybe she'd gotten her hopes up too soon.

The cab pulled to a stop outside Finley's building. Without looking at her, he handed the driver some folded-up bills and got out of the car. Given his cold shoulder, she was surprised when he waited by the door to help her step out and then escorted her into the building with his hand resting at her back.

Taking that as a sign he might be thawing, she ventured, "Wild couple of days, huh?"

He raised a brow, his words barbed. "I thought you didn't do small talk, Satori."

She flinched, his pointed reference to the first memory she returned telling her everything she needed to know.

He was *so* not over it, and things were *far* from settled.

Fucking fantastic.

They hurried through the newly restored lobby, and Finley nodded a curt thanks at the doorman who summoned the elevator for them. Nord and Lina weren't the only ones who'd helped repair the damage Mikel's impromptu visit had caused. With the aid of Crombie's temporal freeze, Quinn had been able to meet with every survivor and strip away their traumatic memories. She'd also modified the memories of the nearby neighbors. It had been a busy couple of days. Now, no one was the wiser that the building had ever been destroyed.

"Have a good evening, you two," the doorman called as they entered the elevator car.

"We will," Quinn said with forced cheerfulness, her eyes lifting up to Finley's profile as her stomach dropped. *Or you know . . . an absolutely miserable one. Same difference, really.*

The ride up to the penthouse was the most awkward one and a half minutes of her life. Every time she thought of something to say, she snapped her mouth shut as soon as she caught a peek at Finley's stony profile.

Maybe if she wasn't feeling quite so exposed by her curse-induced confessions, she would have brazened her way into a confrontation, but she was still hurting over the fact that he hadn't so much as acknowledged that she'd told him she loved him.

Quinn hadn't thought she was the kind of woman who needed to hear her lover reciprocate the words right away, but apparently she was. Having never said 'I love you' to anyone outside her immediate family—Lina included—she'd never been put in a position where the words had been withheld from her before.

She didn't like it.

In fact, this whole silent treatment thing was really starting to piss her off.

The elevator doors slid open with a soft chime, and Finley hurried out, keys already in hand. He didn't even wait for her to get over the threshold before announcing, "I'm going to take a shower."

She gaped at his retreating back, kicking the door closed with more force than was strictly necessary. When even that failed to garner an annoyed glance in her direction, she slumped against it.

"Fuck, what a mess. We've been unofficially official for what . . . two, three days, and already he wants nothing to do with me. Is that some kind of record?"

Despite her mocking words, panic churned inside of her. She did not come this far just to lose everything at the finish line. The trouble was, she didn't know what she was supposed to do. Should she give him the time and space he was obviously searching for, or should she press the issue like she normally would?

Quinn wasn't used to second-guessing herself, but this kind of thing was so far outside her comfort zone she didn't even know where to start. She'd never been in a relationship that lasted more than a single night. Ever. She'd certainly never had to deal with anything like this. Never had to apologize . . . not when it really counted.

Chewing on her lip, Quinn turned to the only source of answers she had at her disposal.

*What would Lina and Nord do?*

As the only healthy, functioning, head-over-heels in love couple she'd seen in action as an adult, the berserkers were her only frame of reference to pull from.

Quinn's lips quirked as the answers came to her. There was no way in hell Nord would let Lina get away with shutting him out. He'd probably pick her up, toss her on the bed, and fuck the anger right out of her.

Seeing as how she lacked the strength to throw Finley around and have her way with him, she'd probably have to settle for the Lina version. Which, come to think of it, boiled down to the same thing. Lina wouldn't let Nord run away either.

No way in hell.

They would stay and work it out. They loved each other too much not to face their problems head-on. Which meant if Quinn really wanted to make a go of this with Finley, she needed to do the same.

After everything they'd been through to be together, she wasn't about to backslide. Either they wanted this, or they didn't—there was no in between—but they owed it to each other to at least try.

With that in mind, she kicked off her shoes and unzipped her skirt, letting the skin-warmed fabric slide down her legs before tugging off her camisole as she made her way down the hall. By the time she reached Finley's room, she was nude, her skirt and silk shirt both draped over her arm. The last thing she wanted was to piss him off further by leaving them lying around.

She'd just picked up on the soft roar of the shower coming from his ensuite when she noted the trail of clothes he'd left strewn on the carpet with a frown. More than anything, that small act spoke to his mental state. Finley *never* left his clothes on the floor. He was disgustingly meticulous about hanging them up or tossing them in the hamper. As long as she'd known him, he'd never left so much as a sock out of place.

That's when Quinn realized she wasn't dealing with temper or a bruised ego. This was so much deeper than that.

Finley was hurting because of her.

Moving slowly so as not to startle him, she stepped into the bathroom, taking a second to appreciate how he looked standing beneath the steamy spray of water. The glass had just started to fog, but she could still perfectly make out his sculpted form, his muscles bunched and tight as he stood with his hands pressed to the tile, head hanging down. Her gaze followed the arc of his spine, down to the two dimples on either side of its base begging her to kiss them, and then lower still to the firm rounded globes of his ass.

She bit her lip at the answering flood of arousal. This was hardly the time for that, but she couldn't help her body's reaction to the perfection of his. Finley was fucking beautiful, every inch of him. Even his feet were attractive, which was pretty much unheard of.

*Focus, Satori. You actually have to make up before you can have the make up sex.*

Without giving herself a chance to chicken out, she moved into the shower behind him, curling her arms around his waist and pressing a kiss to his shoulder before laying her cheek against it.

He stiffened but didn't try to pull away.

"You can't shut me out, Fin. This is supposed to be a celebration." She brushed her fingers over his belly, enjoying the feel of his muscles twitching in response to the featherlight caress as she whispered, "Our first night together."

"But it's not our first night, is it?"

She squeezed her eyes shut against his scathing tone, reminding herself that she'd earned it.

"I told you I was sorry about that."

"Did you? I don't remember hearing an apology."

She sighed heavily, running her hand up the ridges of his abs to rest it just over his heart. "I know you're upset—"

He laughed, low and bitter. "Upset? Princess, you have no fucking idea."

"Then explain it to me so I do."

His knuckles turned white where they flexed over the tile. "I'm not upset. I'm fucking gutted."

"Fin—"

"Just answer one question for me. Why did you do it?"

She swallowed. "I was trying to protect you."

"Bullshit."

"Fin, I swear. If Mikel knew how I felt about you—"

He slammed his fist against the tile, shocking the hell out of her when it cracked under the force. "I don't give a fuck about Mikel. I want to know why you kept it from *me*."

"I just told you."

"No. Not good enough. I had a feeling you'd meddled because I'd been having the strangest déjà vu for weeks, but fuck, Quinn, I never thought you'd sink that low. That you could do that to me. You don't get to steal something that important from me and tell me it was for my own good."

"It was just sex—"

He went rigid in her arms. "Just sex? Are you fucking kidding me? Do you have any idea what you stole from me—from us—when you took away that memory?"

Her heart clenched like it was caving in on itself. She'd never heard him so . . . wounded. She hadn't been prepared for what the sound of his pain would do to her.

"I just . . . I just assumed. It was only one night, I didn't think it mattered . . ."

Each new word out of her mouth only seemed to dig the hole she'd dug for herself deeper. By the time she gave up trying to form a coherent sentence, Finley's body felt as if it was carved out of stone. There wasn't an ounce of softness left in it.

Quinn dropped her arms, thinking she'd made a terrible mistake getting in the shower with him. "I'm sorry," she whispered, turning to leave.

He spun around so fast, she nearly slipped, but he caught her by the back of the neck, his grip firm but not painful.

"You started this, so you don't get to walk away until it's finished," he growled in her ear.

She swallowed convulsively, not liking what the word 'finished' implied.

He pulled her back under the spray, shoving her up against the wall and holding her there with a hand wrapped around her throat. His hold still wasn't tight enough to hurt, but the domination of the act was unmistakable. Finley was in charge, and she had better obey.

She flinched when his grief-darkened eyes met hers. The raw agony in their depths shredded her insides. He held her stare, forcing her to take the full weight of it, forcing her to face the truth of what she'd done to him. Then he started speaking, and the pain in his eyes was nothing compared to the absolute agony in his voice.

"More than anyone else, I should have been able to trust you. I should have been safe with *you*," he growled.

"Fin, you are safe with me."

"How can you say that when you stole everything from me?"

"All I did was take a couple of memories . . ."

"A couple of memories?" he snarled. "You stole my reason for existing."

"W-what?"

"Like you don't know."

"I don't, Fin. I swear I don't know what you're talking about."

"Don't lie to me."

"I'm not, I promise."

"You were the one playing around in my head. How could you not know?"

"I never looked at your memories after I removed them. I didn't want to hear your thoughts. I didn't want to know what you felt about that night, or for me. It was hard enough resisting you with my own memories. It would have been impossible if I carried the weight of yours too."

He blinked at her, his expression still severe, but starting to crack at the edges. "You didn't?"

She shook her head.

"You bloody little fool." He kissed her then, hard and rough. It was a struggle to breathe as he branded her with his lips. He pulled back far too soon, his forehead pressed to hers, hair plastered to his skull, eyes blazing.

She opened her mouth, but he pressed a finger to her lips. "No, princess. I'm going to talk now, and you're going to listen."

She nodded, heart racing.

"It's not going to be pretty for either of us. There's a reason I don't speak about these things, let alone share them, but you need to hear all of it to understand."

"O-okay. I'm ready."

He closed his eyes, drawing a deep breath through his nose before he started talking. She knew whatever he was about to tell her was going to be bad if he needed to brace himself before even starting. When his eyes opened again, the warm hazel was practically eclipsed by the black, but that did nothing to tame the ghosts lurking there. If anything, it showcased them more clearly.

Finley was walking a dark path right now, the jagged edges of his soul visible in every harsh breath and tense line of his body.

Not knowing what else to do, Quinn pulled a hand up and rested it over the one still wrapped around her throat. A muscle fluttered in his jaw at the touch, and he finally started to speak.

"There's a reason I waited so long to lose my virginity, why I don't go casually from partner to partner, why I *need* control. I don't do 'just sex,' Quinn. I need to trust someone before I can be intimate with them. I have to be selective because I need to feel safe. And even then, I don't let myself get too close. I have to rely on dominance to maintain the boundaries I need." He started to tremble beneath her touch, and that's when she realized the drops splashing down his cheeks were tears.

"Fin—"

He gritted his teeth, talking over her. Forcing the words out like he was walking on shards of glass. Each one brittle and filled with pain.

"I spent years fighting off the advances of men and women who promised me the world if only I would sell my body. Such a small price to pay for a full belly and roof over my head. It was only a little thing they wanted, after all. My innocence, my self-worth, my fucking soul."

Every word carved her wide open. If she could look away from him right now, she was pretty sure she'd find a river of her blood dripping into the pool of their tears. She'd guessed as much about his past, after what she'd seen in his mind. But hearing the truth colored by his pain, God, it was so much worse.

"And I spent even more years fighting those who wanted to take what I wouldn't willingly give. Even when there wasn't a chance in hell I could beat them, I kept fighting. Even when I was starving, I'd have rather been beaten and bloody than raped. I've had my bones broken and my face bashed in more times than I can count. I don't think I slept properly once the entire time I lived on those streets. I knew if I did, I'd wake up to find myself buggered or worse, and I'd fought too hard to let that happen. That day, the one with the door, I didn't have any fight left. I was so damn hungry . . ."

Her throat was so thick with emotion, it felt like she'd swallowed a knife. It took her three times to get his name out. "Finley."

"No, I need you to hear this. You need to know, so you'll finally understand."

Quinn had a feeling the worst was yet to come. But she nodded, forcing herself to hold his shattered gaze. "Tell me."

"I'd never taken someone home . . . not the first night. And I wouldn't . . . I wouldn't have, but you were . . ." He sucked in a breath, his entire body shaking now.

Quinn wrapped her arms around him, needing to hold him. To offer him comfort however she could.

"I was what?"

"You were the one person in all of existence who should have been my safe harbor. The one person I could trust without question. The one who was always supposed to protect my heart."

"Finley, of course I'll protect it."

He shook his head, his eyes squeezing closed.

"But you didn't. I gave it to you then and there at the District. You didn't even know what you had. But I did. I did."

His eyes flew open, and she forgot how to breathe at the sight of the raw pain there. The ghosts were gone but only to be replaced by a new hurt, the one she'd caused. *This.* Whatever he was about to say next was why he was so upset with her.

"You're mine, Quinn. You were made for me, and I for you. Two halves of one soul, separated by time and space, brought together by fate. So many soulmates never get the chance we were given. So many wander alone, never to know true completion, but not us. We were blessed, just like Nord and Lina. We should have had what they do, but you robbed us both. When you took away that night, you didn't just take a memory. You ripped out a part of my soul. But not just that, you took away the moment of knowing. That soul-deep clarity I felt when I recognized you as *mine*. You broke me before I had a chance to realize I was being broken. And then you forced me to walk around for the next two years searching for what

I'd lost. Searching for the missing piece of my soul without realizing that the entire time, you were right there standing in front of me."

It was too much. His pain was too much. She couldn't breathe, could hardly see through her tears. She wished she could go back. She wished she could do it all over. If she'd known what it would cost them, she never would have done it.

"I'm sorry, Finley. I'm so sorry."

He kissed her, just a soft press of his lips over hers. She could taste his tears. He was crying openly now, his voice tortured as he continued.

"I never thought I would feel safe enough with anyone to let my guard down. To give them more than just my body, which I could only do on my terms. And then I found you. My miracle. My reward for every shit awful thing I've had to endure in my life. My fucking purpose, and you took it away."

"Finley," she whispered, her voice ragged. She didn't think she could take any more.

"That moment that you thought was nothing? The night that was just sex to you? That's the night I found my reason for being alive. I used to wonder, you know. Why I didn't die out there. Why someone didn't just kill me and put me out of my misery. The Brotherhood taught me that Guardians had a purpose. That one day, if we were lucky, we'd discover it, and everything would make perfect sense. And then I saw you and I knew, Quinn, I fucking knew. I was made for you, to be yours. And. You. Took. It. Away."

"I didn't . . . I didn't know. Fin, you have to b-believe me." She was crying so hard she was hiccupping, his face blurred by her tears. It would have hurt less if he ripped her heart straight out of her chest. It belonged to him anyway; he could have it if that's what it took to fix things. "I'm sorry. I'm so so sorry."

He pulled her into him, crushing her into his body as they held each other, both mourning the loss of something she could never ever repair. She'd returned the memory, but realizing what she'd stolen, understanding how deeply she'd wounded him, she didn't think there was any way she could ever make up for that.

Finley had trusted her on the spot, for the first time in his life, because he believed she'd be the one person to never hurt him. And after a lifetime of searching, the second he'd finally felt safe, she'd stolen that peace from him.

"What can I do?" she whispered.

He shook his head. "I don't know. Knowing you weren't purposely keeping the truth of what we are to each other from me is a start."

"Do you think you can ever forgive me?"

He cupped her cheek, his stormy eyes searching hers. "I already have."

"But how? How can you after what I did?"

"Because I love you. I was born to love you."

As badly as she'd wanted to hear the words earlier, she felt so unworthy of his love in that moment it physically pained her to hear him say it.

"I won't lie to you, sweetheart. It still hurts. Forgiving you doesn't undo the damage, but I see now that you didn't do it intentionally. That goes a long way to ease the ache."

"No, Fin. I don't deserve to get off that easily. You need to punish me. Hurt me like I hurt you. Please. I need to be punished so that I can make it right. So I'm worthy of your forgiveness."

He jerked back. "What?"

"I took away something you desperately needed, and now you need to take it back. So tie me up, spank me, use one of those floggers of yours. Call me every awful, vile name in the book. I don't care. Do whatever you need to do to me until you feel like we're even. I hurt you, Finley, so please, if it will make things right between us, hurt me. Use my body however you need to. I want you to feel in control again. I need you to feel as safe with me as I feel with you."

"Sweetheart . . ." He cupped her cheeks, shaking his head. "That's not how it works. Any punishment I deliver will be agreed upon in advance and earned, but I will never raise a hand to you in anger. Not in or outside of the bedroom."

"But I did earn it. I hurt you so badly. I need to fix it. Please let me fix it. I can't lose you."

His expression softened further. "Maybe you did, but the things that are broken between us can't be mended that way."

Her heart cracked in half hearing that he thought they were broken. He'd once told her they'd never be over, had what she'd done made him change his mind?

"But if it will help—"

"I said no."

"Please, I just want to make it right. I'll do anything."

"Anything?"

She nodded, tears still falling freely.

"Then I want you to make me a vow, here and now."

"A vow? You'd trust my word?"

He looked her dead in the eye as he slowly dipped his chin in a nod. "I do because I'm going to tell you exactly what will happen if I ever find out you've gone back on it."

She shivered, his meaning clear even if he hadn't spoken the words aloud. If she broke her promise, things really would be over between them. This was her only chance.

"I won't. I swear."

He ran his thumb over her bottom lip. "You'd better not, princess. It would break my heart to walk away from you, but it would hurt more spending my life with a woman I couldn't trust. I know now that you didn't realize what you'd done, but any meddling from here on out is a knowing betrayal."

Her lip trembled at just the thought of him leaving her.

Holding her gaze, he said, "No more messing around in my head. Ever. If I want to open my mind up to you, that is my choice, and I will initiate it, but you don't get to play God with my memories ever again. They are off-limits."

"I won't. I promise, Finley. Never again."

"Good."

He reached over and shut off the shower. Then he lifted her in his arms, cradling her close to his body.

"What are you doing?"

"A do-over."

"What?"

"I want a do-over. You took away our first night, so now we're going to do it over. And this time, I expect it to end the way it's supposed to."

# CHAPTER NINETEEN
## FINLEY

As he carried Quinn to his bed, Finley couldn't get past the imagery. Cradled as she was in his arms, she felt like his bride. In lots of ways, she was. He'd laid his heart at her feet. She'd given him her vow. They'd bared their souls to one another.

It was the rawest, most vulnerable Finley had ever been with another human being. He knew it was the same for her. And while he may never be able to give her all the brutal details of his past, there was no denying she was intimately familiar with every broken, scarred part of him after their confrontation in the shower. The only one who ever would be.

Now it was time for them to do the same with their bodies.

They were both feeling exposed, and dare he say, fragile. But the only way back to solid ground was through each other. By proving through touch what they'd already declared in words. Only this time, Finley didn't want to hide behind games or power dynamics.

He wanted to make love to her.

It was something he'd never done, never allowed himself to do. Even when he'd found partners he trusted, he'd never given them that final piece of himself. The piece he now knew he'd been saving for Quinn.

He wanted her. All of her.

In exchange, he wanted to give her all of him.

And by the time they were done, he wanted her so thoroughly imprinted on his soul that if anyone ever dared tried to strip her away from him again, it would be an impossible feat.

Quinn shivered in his arms as the cool air washed over her wet skin.

"Let me grab you a towel," he murmured, carefully setting her down on the mattress.

Her hand snaked out to grab his wrist, a look of panic flashing in her eyes. One he recognized for what it was.

Tenderness shot through him. She was afraid. After everything they'd been through, she was more terrified than ever he would leave her and never come back. Especially now that she'd finally torn down the last of her walls. Unfortunately, time would be the only way to truly erase her fear and prove that he wasn't going anywhere.

Still, Finley offered her what reassurance he could. He smoothed a palm over her hair, watching thick drops of water splash down her back and onto the blanket. "It's okay, princess. I'll be right back."

She released him with a wary nod, biting down on her plump lower lip as she did.

Finley pulled it free with his thumb, replacing the sharp sting of her teeth with a featherlight kiss. "I promise. You're naked in my bed, Satori. There's nowhere else I'd rather be, except perhaps inside you."

Her eyes fluttered closed, the spikes of her eyelashes tangling together as a delicate shiver worked its way down her body. "Hurry."

Finley moved fast but could feel her deep purple gaze on him the entire way. When he returned to the bedroom with a plush towel in hand, Quinn wasn't on the bed. His heart stuttered, lungs seizing. But then he caught a flash of her raven-colored hair, and he stopped breathing for a different reason.

While he'd been gone, she'd climbed off the bed and moved to kneel on the floor. Her eyes were down, thighs spread wide, arms behind her back. For a woman offering submission, she looked like a fucking goddess.

He had to force himself to draw in air as arousal punched him straight in the gut.

"What are you doing, princess?" he asked, moving back into the room until he was standing in front of her.

"If you have to ask, then I must be doing it wrong."

His lips twitched at the sulky undertone in her voice. He reached out, tipping her chin up and forcing her to meet his gaze. "I already told you I wasn't going to punish you, Quinn."

"I know, but . . . isn't this what you need?" she asked, her cheeks turning a deep pink.

Finley crouched down so they were level. "If by *this* you mean you, then yes, you're exactly what I need. But if you mean your submission, then no, I don't need it."

Something flickered in the back of her eyes.

*Was that disappointment?*

He wrapped his hand around the wet length of her hair and gave it a soft tug, jerking her chin up higher. "Do you want me to dominate you, princess?"

She swallowed, and her pupils expanded, the black nearly eclipsing the purple. "Yes, Daddy."

Finley's cock gave an approving jerk.

Quinn let out a nearly inaudible moan as he trailed his fingertips up her inner thigh and leaned forward, pressing his lips to her ear. "Too bad. I have different plans in mind tonight." He gave her pussy a light tap, and her hips bucked forward as she cried out. "Stand up."

Her breathing was uneven as she rose to her feet. "You're acting pretty bossy for a guy who just shot me down when I offered him control."

Finley bit back a laugh. "Or maybe, by denying you, I gave you exactly what you were asking for, Satori."

She raised a brow. "How do you figure?"

"Can you think of a more fitting punishment for a brat than telling her no?"

"I guess not." She tipped her head to the side and gave him a considering look.

"What?"

"You're better at this Dom thing than I thought."

"Did you picture it often, Satori?"

It was the kind of question she usually avoided, but not this time. This time, she blushed as she admitted, "More than I care to admit."

His eyes swept over her body, lingering on her tightly furled nipples and the deepening flush across her skin. Her breath stuttered under his blatant regard, and she pressed her trembling thighs together. He loved how responsive she was, how badly she craved him, even when he'd barely touched her.

"And why do you think the reality is better?"

"You make me actually enjoy ceding control."

His grin stretched as he picked up the towel that had fallen to the floor and set to work drying her hair. "That is the point of a power exchange."

"That may be the point, but it's not always the reality. The difference with you is I know you're going to take care of me no matter what. Even when you're upset or disappointed with me." Her eyes darted away from his as she whispered, "Even when I don't deserve it."

Finley sat down beside her. "Look at me, Quinn."

She let out a frustrated sigh but obeyed.

"No matter what happens, or how many rows we have—because let's face it, the two of us are going to butt heads—"

She chuckled and nodded in agreement.

He cupped her cheek, his thumb sweeping across her cheekbone. "But even then, sweetheart, taking care of you is my number one priority. There will never come a day when that won't be true. But even more than that—I need you to really hear this, are you listening?"

She nodded, her eyes swimming with tears.

Holding her gaze, he gave her the rest of his truth. "You, my stubborn and infuriating Quinn, you deserve to be taken care of. To be loved. No matter what. The times when you feel like you don't are when you need it the most. And on those days, I will be at your side reminding you just how worthy you are."

"Fin." She didn't manage more than that before her lips were on his, telling him everything she couldn't verbalize with her kiss.

He threaded his fingers through her hair, pouring just as much unspoken emotion into it as she did, but he pulled back and rested his forehead against hers before they could get carried away.

"Is anything else weighing on you right now? Anything you need clarity on or want to talk to me about?"

She shook her head, her expression soft with affection.

"Good. Then I can finally get to work showing you how much I love you."

She smiled, but it wobbled at the edges. "Isn't that what you've been doing this whole time?"

"With every breath I take, Satori. Glad you finally noticed."

"Oh, I noticed. I just didn't let myself believe it. But I'm done lying to myself—and to you. I've been in love with you since the first time I laid eyes on you, Fin. As much as I denied my feelings, I never got over you, and I never will. One look and you were it for me. And then you found your way back to me, and I had to pretend like we'd never met . . . It nearly killed me trying to stay away from you. I picked fights with you because it was the only safe way to get your attention, but what I really wanted was this."

She pressed her hand flat to his chest.

"My body?"

"Your heart, Batman."

"It's yours, princess. It's always been yours."

This time, when he kissed her, he pressed her back onto the bed, keeping his weight braced on his arms as he settled between her legs and savored her mouth.

She rocked up into him, one of her hands fisted in his hair, the other dragging down his back. "Fin, please. I need you."

"Not yet. I rushed things with us once before. I realize now what a mistake that was. I should have taken my time. Memorized you until I knew your body well enough to recognize it by touch alone. I intend to rectify that mistake."

She whimpered as he started to trail kisses down her neck and trace random patterns along the inside of one of her arms and then skate them over her ribcage.

Quinn squirmed beneath him, shamelessly working her hips over him, trying to get him to slide inside her.

"Naughty girl," he whispered, his thumb just barely grazing the underside of one of her breasts.

"Please, Fin. I've waited so long for this."

"And I haven't?"

"You didn't know what you were missing—I did."

He stopped and pulled back to look at her. "I'd rethink your line of persuasion if I were you."

A guilty flush stained her cheeks. "It's true, though."

Finley couldn't help but smile. "I suppose it is. Consider waiting just another part of that punishment you begged for."

Challenge flashed in her eyes, and she moved her hand so it was curled around his rigid length. "I want to come around your cock, Fin. I want you buried deep inside me where you belong. And then I want you to pump me so full of your cum I can feel it dripping out. Don't you want that too?"

Finley nearly blew in her hand from her words alone. He saw stars when Quinn brushed the pad of her thumb over his weeping tip, rubbing the pearly beads of precum along his swollen shaft. But instead of giving in, it only steeled his resolve.

"I'm prepared to give you everything you want and then some, sweetheart. But make no mistake, by the time I'm through with you, you're not going to come. You're going to fucking arrive."

Her mouth fell open, and she had to blink a few times before she could refocus on him. "Jesus, Fin."

*That's more like it.*

He set to work on his task, exploring every inch of her body, making her writhe with need, punishing her with pleasure. Each time he ran his hands over her velvety skin, he'd echo the caress with his lips and tongue. Sometimes even with a soft scrape of his teeth. He started innocently, brushing the pads of his thumbs over her eyebrows and smoothing out the furrow between them with a kiss. Then he ghosted his fingers along the shell of her ear, whispering her name before biting down on the soft lobe.

On and on it went, his hands preceding his mouth as he worked his way down her body. By the time he reached her belly button, she was openly cursing him.

"Dammit, Batman. Stop playing with me."

"But you're my favorite toy."

She bared her teeth and made a sound he assumed was supposed to be a growl. She reminded him more of a grumpy kitten.

"Shh, just relax. Let me love you."

Her expression immediately softened, and she flopped her head back on the pillow with a groan. "Fine. At least you're closing in on the good bits."

Finley raised a brow, but she didn't notice with the way her arm was currently flung over her eyes.

*Oh, princess, you don't even know what you've done, do you?*

He smirked to himself as he ran his palm over her belly, but instead of cupping her aching center, he trailed his fingers along the inside of one of her thighs. And when he moved so his shoulders were nestled between her legs, his other hand mirrored the touch on her other thigh.

Her body relaxed, her legs widening further, and he chuckled to himself when he denied her yet again and moved lower to start paying attention to the backs of her knees.

He was enjoying himself immensely, noting the things that made her gasp or go boneless. It was harder than he cared to admit to ignore the slick folds begging for his attention.

*Soon.*

"Finley," she whined when he reached her ankles and started to massage the arches of her feet. "Please. I'm doing my best to be patient here, but consider this me sending up the bat signal. I need you, Batman."

"This is you being patient?"

She sat up on her elbows and glared down the length of her body at him. Well, it should have been a glare. It lacked the necessary sting with as hooded and desire-glazed as her eyes were.

"If you don't take your Batmobile and park it in my Batcave, we're going to have words."

Finley barked out a laugh as he curled his hands around her ankles and slid them up over her calves. "Is that so, princess?"

She gave him an emphatic nod.

"And what, pray tell, is it you'd say to me?"

"That you're fired."

"Would you really fire me? That seems to be counterproductive when my end goal is giving you exactly what you want."

His hands rested on top of her thighs, his thumbs just barely brushing the sensitive skin of her bikini line. Her legs trembled beneath his light hold.

"Fin, touch me," she begged.

"I am touching you. Quite thoroughly."

"You know what I mean."

He adjusted his position, shoulders once again braced between her legs, his face inches away from her drenched core. Finley licked his lips, the proof of her need for him a delicious temptation.

Quinn moaned. "Me, Finley. You're supposed to lick *me*."

He chuckled, his breath washing across her overheated skin and making her shiver.

"God, I could come just from that."

Finley deliberately blew on her clit, watching her body chase the phantom touch, silently demanding more.

"What sort of sex voodoo are you doing down there? Jesus," she panted, her hands grasping his head and attempting to tug him forward. "I've never been so close without direct stimulation before."

He smirked at her. "Next time, we'll have to see if I can make you come with words alone. Or maybe just by playing with your gorgeous nipples. I know how much you love it when I tease them." His smile stretched. "Though you really lose your mind when I get a little rough. Do you enjoy the sting of pain alongside your pleasure, princess?"

"Fuck, Fin. I'd enjoy it if you tickled me at this point. Just so long as your hands are on me, you can do whatever you want."

He tested her theory, dancing his fingers over her pretty pink cunt and grinning when her hips bucked up off the bed.

"So responsive."

"Like that's a surprise? You've been edging me for hours."

"It hasn't been hours."

"No, it's been two fucking years."

"And whose fault is that?"

"Mine," she moaned as he flicked her swollen bundle of nerves. "It's mine."

*Oh yes, she enjoyed the pain just as much as the pleasure.* Finley's eyes dipped to the fresh flood of slick the single strike had triggered. *Maybe more.* The knowledge made his cock throb with need.

"I'm going to give you what you want now, princess. You've been such a good girl."

She whimpered as he slid two fingers into her and worked them slowly in and out.

"But I don't want you to come yet. I want you to wait until I'm inside you so we can fall apart together. Can you do that? Can you be my good girl a little while longer?"

"Y-yes," she stuttered, hips meeting each slow glide of his fingers.

"Yes, what?"

Quinn's eyes shot open, meeting his. Her breath hitched at whatever she found in his gaze. Color suffused her cheeks, turning them a deep rose.

"Yes, Daddy."

Her entire body relaxed as she gave him the words, like that small act of submission was what she'd been waiting for. Like she'd needed it. That's when Finley realized that power exchange and making love weren't mutually exclusive. He could give her both. With the way they felt about each other, he could fuck her raw, and it would still be making love, so long as their hearts were involved.

Finley continued to work her with his fingers, keeping his strokes slow and measured and only ceasing once he'd brought her to the brink.

Then he did it again with his tongue.

This time, he stopped when he felt the telltale tremors in her legs and heard the soft whine beneath her sweet moans.

"Are you ready for me to be inside you, princess?"

"I'm so past ready there isn't a word for it." She was trembling, her porcelain skin rosy and covered in goosebumps from him teasing.

He grinned. "You're still coherent. It can't be all that bad."

She flipped him off as he got to his knees and took his cock in his hand, lining himself up with her opening.

"That's the plan, Satori."

He prolonged that first full slide, holding her gaze and watching her pulse thunder in time with his as he sank inch after delicious inch. It was a struggle against his own control not to drive all the way home. As much as he'd been teasing her, he'd done the same to himself. His balls were so tight he worried he may not be able to make it good for her. But then, if he'd done his job right, she probably wouldn't last long herself.

"Fuck, Quinn," he grunted as soon as he was planted all the way. She was gripping him tighter than a fucking fist. "You feel so fucking good, princess."

She moaned her agreement, and he would have sworn he felt the vibrations of her affirmation rumble straight up his cock. He couldn't stay still after that, though somehow—divine intervention perhaps —he managed to keep his thrusts slow and languid.

Quinn didn't seem to mind. She was lost to her pleasure now, biting down on her lower lip as she struggled not to tumble right over the edge. She crushed her body against his as he leaned down to kiss her, echoing the slow drive of his hips with his tongue.

"This is how it should have been that first time, princess. No games. No barriers. Just you and me. Souls, bodies, and hearts aligned, returning to each other."

"Yes," she agreed, squeezing him tighter, her nails sinking into his skin as she clung to him.

"I love you, Quinn. With all that I am, I love you."

She blinked back tears, her throat working hard as she tried to find her voice. "You're the only man I've ever loved, Fin. You're it for me."

He picked up his pace then, rocking into her slick heat with enough force to send the headboard crashing into the wall.

"Now, princess. Come for me."

She needed no further encouragement. Quinn cried out his name, nails clawing down his back as she bowed up off the bed. As soon as she started to come, her inner walls clamped down hard around him, milking him and sending him toppling over the edge right alongside her.

Ears ringing, heart galloping in his chest, all Finley could do was rest his forehead against hers while they both came back down. He had no way of knowing how much time had passed before he heard her tentatively call his name.

"Fin?"

"Hmm?"

"Does our do-over include the things you said to me? You know . . . after?"

He forced his eyes open. She looked so fucking vulnerable, peering up at him. Her irises were nearly violet and filled with such hope and love he felt like his heart might explode from the beauty of it.

It took him a second to shift his thoughts from her back to the lost memory. Realizing what she was asking for, that she wanted a do-over of her own, Finley slid out of her, silently mourning the loss as he rolled onto his back. He pulled her with him, curling her into his side until her head rested on his chest and her leg was thrown over his hip.

Kissing her temple, he gave her what she needed. "You're mine now, Quinn. My good girl. I'm never letting you go."

A tear splashed against his chest as she snuggled closer and let out a watery sigh. "I never thought I'd get to hear you say that again, but I desperately wanted to, Batman." She tipped her head up so she was looking at him when she confessed, "The only thing I ever wanted to be is yours."

Heart too full for words, Finley banded his arms tighter around her, cupping a hand around the side of her head and pressing another kiss to her forehead. Pressure built at the back of his eyes, but he didn't realize it had burst free until Quinn stiffened in his arms.

"Are you crying? Shit, I'm sorry. I shouldn't have brought that night back up—"

"Shh, princess. They're happy tears," he admitted, his voice rough with emotion as he held her. The little furrow that worked its way between her brows told him she wasn't sure she believed him, so as he kissed it away, he added, "That's all I ever wanted too."

# CHAPTER TWENTY
## FINLEY

A soft sob tore him from a sleep so deep he didn't immediately know where he was. When the second one came right on its heels, his body went rigid with fear.

*Quinn.*

He knifed upright, adrenaline chasing away his mental fog. Finley drew on his power, seamlessly turning the sheet beneath his hand into a weapon as his eyes swept the room. Given the desperate and tortured sound of her cries, he'd half expected to find a shadowy figure looming over her thrashing body, but one look determined that her monsters weren't of the corporeal variety.

Her eyes were squeezed shut, beads of sweat dotting her forehead as she brokenly began chanting in her sleep.

"No. Nononono. Not again."

*Nightmares.*

Finley's heart slowed, and he let out a heavy breath as he set his gun aside, his relief at finding her safe diminished by her obvious suffering.

"Quinn," he called softly, reaching out to brush away the sweat-damp locks of hair off her face. "Sweetheart, you're dreaming."

Instead of pulling her out of her dreams, his voice only seemed to torment her further.

"Fin. No, Fin. Please. Don't leave me."

His blood ran cold as he realized what memory her twisted dreams had trapped her in. For one horrifying second, Finley wondered if this was more than a dream. If it could be a side effect of the curse, or worse, if Mikel's vile magic had ensnared her once more.

The possibility alone was enough to spur Finley to action. He couldn't allow her to suffer like this, not if there was something he could do about it. He'd never attempted what he was about to, he'd never been close enough to someone to consider it, but lack of experience wasn't about to stop him. Nor was the very real threat of what the Brotherhood would do to him if they found out. He'd deal with the consequences later. Right now, the only thing that mattered was her.

Finley called on his power, turning his bedroom into a shimmering web of gold as the threads of reality revealed themselves. When his eyes landed on Quinn, he let out a shocked gasp.

He'd accessed his magic in her presence plenty of times, but this was the first time since realizing who and what she was to him. No one had prepared him for how it would change, well, everything.

Instead of the usual golden hue, Quinn shone a blinding iridescent white. She could have been made of the stars themselves, such was her glow. It physically hurt to look at her, but Finley couldn't make himself turn away. He was helpless against her pull; he couldn't have resisted it if he wanted to. And the last thing he wanted right now was to resist.

She was a beacon drawing him forward, guiding him back home. Back to her.

He knew how the Guardian connections were forged, but only in theory. So it was pure reflex driving him as he reached out, his hands trembling as he carefully plucked the strand he needed and wove it into one of his own.

Electric heat washed through him the second the ephemeral fibers came into contact, and his mind was immediately filled with the chaotic buzz of her thoughts. Her voice was so loud in his mind she was practically screaming.

He gritted his teeth, swallowing back his own agonized cry as he forced himself to focus on his task. A mistake now could very well be the end of them both. He had no choice but to work through the unexpected pain and pray he didn't lose himself under the assault of her tormented mind. It was a task that grew harder as he went on and her feelings seeped through, merging with his own until it was impossible to tell if the desperate clawing in his chest was her panic or his own.

Time was a foreign concept as he wove the very threads of their essence, tying them together. It wasn't technically permanent; what was woven could be undone, but never without both parties being irrevocably damaged. Because of him, their bodies and minds were now extensions of each other, just like their souls. He would always feel her inside him, and she him.

They were bound. Not just by danger or fate, but all the way down to the invisible current that gave them life.

Finley was covered in sweat and visibly shaking by the time he was done. The forging hadn't just been tough on him physically; he'd nearly depleted his reservoir in the process. Knowing he still needed his magic for what was to come, he cut off the flow of his power. The immediate dampening of his senses helped to somewhat mute Quinn's agony, but he didn't think anything would take away the lingering echo of her screams.

The need to go to her, to protect her, surged through his veins, but he knew he'd be no good to her in his current state. He was too rattled by the taste of her fear. He needed to get control of himself before diving back into the fray.

Running a hand through his hair, body humming with tension, Finley focused on taking first one breath and then the next, until his heart rate returned to something resembling a normal pace once more. Only then did he allow himself to turn back to Quinn.

Connected as they now were, it was easy for Finley to open up the mental link between them and follow the bridge until his consciousness was fully immersed with hers. Once there, he could see, hear, and feel everything she did.

"Quinn!" he called as soon as he spotted her. But she didn't hear him, his words swallowed whole by the storm raging all around them.

She was kneeling in a pool of blood and lying beside her, bleeding out, was his lifeless body. The sight of it rocked him, taking his mind and bending it in on itself until it was a struggle for him to remain upright.

Finley had once wondered what it would feel like to come face to face with his corpse. Now he knew and immediately wished he could forget. There was nothing quite like being presented with the truth of your mortality to remind you how insignificant you truly were.

But worse, far worse, was the torment etched on Quinn's face as she grieved him. Despite all the memories they'd shared trapped in Mikel's mind prison, this was one he'd yet to experience. At least not from her point of view.

He'd thought the things he'd experienced during the forging had been awful, but that was nothing compared to the full, undiluted reality. It was enough to send a lesser man to his knees. But Finley would endure anything to save her, even bear the full weight of her terror and grief. He'd carry it all for her if he could. Every abhorrent, soul-crushing piece.

He stepped forward, intent on doing just that when the scene before him flickered and peeled away like wispy strands of candy floss. When he blinked, the scene had been reset. Quinn now stood on the far side of the vineyard while he was running toward her like a bat out of hell with two Animagi hot on his heels.

His heart turned over as he realized what was happening.

It was a loop.

Quinn's nightmare forced her to watch him die over and over again.

*Christ.* He had to put an end to this.

His first instinct was to intercept her, but when he tried to catch her and hide the gruesome scene playing out behind him, she ran straight through his body as if he was no more solid than a ghost. He turned in time to watch her collapse to her knees beside his impaled twin. With nothing else for it, he followed behind her, brain scrambling to come up with some way to break through the cycle she was trapped in.

Up until now, the storm had drowned out most of her words, but as he dropped down beside her, he had no trouble making them out.

"Fin . . . Fin, you need to wake up. Please wake up." Quinn's voice cracked, tears rolling down her cheeks and onto his face as she bent herself in half to press her forehead to his. "Come back to me. You have promises to keep. Please, Batman. Don't leave me. Not now. Not . . . not like this. Please, Fin. Please. I love you."

His heart cracked in two, his chest feeling as though it had been ripped open as he listened to her raw, broken pleas.

He'd already forgiven her, but if any part of him was still harboring a grudge over what she'd done, it ended in that moment. This was not a woman who'd been playing games or toying with his emotions. This was a woman who'd just lost everything, who'd been forced to watch as the dreams she had for her future vanished right before her eyes. This was a woman who loved him with the full might of everything she was.

*His* woman.

"Quinn," he groaned, grasping her face tenderly and lifting it up to meet his.

This time, his touch connected. She blinked up at him. "F-Fin?"

"I'm right here. I'm not leaving."

"B-but you're dead."

"No, I'm not. You're dreaming, love. This is all a terrible dream."

"It's not a dream when it really happened."

He took her hand, weaving his fingers through hers as he pressed them over his heart. "Do you feel that?"

Still looking uncertain, she nodded.

"I'm alive. I'm here with you. We're safe now."

She started to crane her neck to look down at the body twitching beside them, but he grasped her chin and forced her to keep her gaze locked on his.

"Don't. Just focus on me and the feel of my heart beating beneath your palm."

Tears continued to swim in her eyes as she stared up at him. "I can't forget. No matter how hard I try, I can't forget watching you die."

"I know, sweetheart."

"I don't want you to die, Fin. I don't want to be alone anymore."

"You aren't alone, princess. You'll never be alone again, I swear it."

Her face crumpled and she sagged against him, sobbing as he held her. "Please don't leave me. I can survive anything but losing you."

"I won't. I promise you, Quinn, I'm not going anywhere. I'm actually incredibly hard to kill. I know that's tough to believe, given what you witnessed, but even without Nord healing me, I would have eventually recovered. I wouldn't be much of a Guardian if I could be taken out so easily."

Quinn made a hiccupping sound halfway between a sob and a laugh, and then she started crying harder. As she fell apart in his arms, Finley realized what he needed to do. If anything had happened the way it was supposed to, he would have done it already, but they had a knack for doing things backward.

He gently pushed her away, brushing a lock of hair behind her ear. "Quinn, love, I need you to wake up now. There's something we need to take care of, but not here."

She sniffled and blinked at him. "I don't know how."

Cupping her cheek, he kissed her nose and then feathered a kiss over her lips. "Just open your eyes."

"If it was that easy, don't you think I would have done it by now?" she grumped, stealing another kiss.

He laughed even as he kissed her back. "There's the ballbuster I know and love."

She let out an offended huff and then ruined the effect by smiling. "Maybe we should just stay here and make out. We can deal with the rest in the morning."

As soon as her lips brushed against his, Finley felt himself being pulled from her mind, his bedroom crystalizing around him as he came back to reality.

Beside him, Quinn sat up with a low groan. "Why is it so easy to wake up when a dream just starts to get good, but never in the middle of a nightmare?"

He skimmed her jaw with his fingers. "Do you want my philosophical take on it, or was that a rhetorical question?"

She shot him a sideways glance. "Save your philosophy until after I've had coffee, Batman."

The patently Quinn response, equal parts feminine exasperation and sarcastic barb, was a welcome relief. After what he'd witnessed in her mind, he'd needed the proof that she was the same indomitable force she'd always been.

She rolled so her head was pillowed in his lap, her gaze trained away from him as she asked, "Why is this still happening? I thought we dealt with the curse."

"Magic leaves a trace, it might take a while to be fully rid of it, or . . ."

"Or?"

He blew out a breath as he gave her the truth. "Or it may never set you free. Either way, I'll always be here to pull you out of the shadows and back into the light." And then, straight down their newly forged bond, he whispered, "*I will protect you from every threat, real or imaginary. From this day forward, it's my life for yours. No matter the cost."*

Quinn stiffened at the sound of his voice in her mind. "Fin . . . why are you speaking to me with your Guardian magic?"

*"It's not my magic, princess. It's our link."*

She looked up at him, her eyes wide as she tentatively sent him her reply. *"But I thought the part where Nate connected our minds was a trick of the curse."*

*"It was."*

*"Then how?"*

He smirked. "Me."

"Finley . . ."

"Don't expect me to apologize. You were lost to the dreams, and I couldn't reach you through normal means. It called for drastic measures."

"And you didn't think to just use your Guardian abilities to reach me like last time?"

"I wanted something more permanent," he admitted, twining their fingers together. "In case we ever found ourselves in this position again." He risked a glance at her face, pleased to see that she looked amused instead of annoyed. *"And I seem to recall you enjoyed the perks of such a connection."*

A lovely flush tinged her cheeks. "It has its uses," she murmured. Then, sighing, she added, "Thank you for coming in after me. Again."

"I'll always come after you."

Her eyes went soft with affection and then bright with curiosity. "What was that you said to me before? I was so distracted by your voice in my mind, I didn't catch the actual words."

His lips twitched. "I wondered. It's not like you to let such declarations go unchecked."

She raised a brow, pushing herself up so that she was facing him, her bent leg resting across his thighs. "Declaration, huh? Sounds important."

"It was more of a vow, actually," he said, folding his arms behind his head and leaning back against the headboard.

"A vow?"

The lack of recognition in her voice made him ask, "How much do you know about a Guardian's vow?"

"Everything I learned about the Brotherhood is tainted by the Council's low opinion of them. So unless it's something Lina mentioned in passing, there's not a whole lot I know that I trust to be unbiased or accurate."

Finley laughed. "Well, without going into a full history lesson—"

"History is worse than philosophy, so please no, definitely not before coffee. Or even after the coffee, honestly . . ."

He placed a finger over her lips to silence her rambling tirade. "Guardians take their vows very seriously."

"Guardians take everything seriously," she said, eyes sparkling with mischief as she licked the finger still resting over her lips.

"Yes, well, you would too if you knew the stakes."

That piqued her curiosity. "What do you mean?"

"Guardians are bound by their promises. They aren't given lightly. In fact, in most cases, there are only two vows a Guardian ever swears. The first, to the Brotherhood, and the second they pledge to the one they are soul-bound to protect."

"Their purpose," Quinn said, her voice soft and her eyes warm.

"It's a vow so sacred, it's only made once in a Guardian's lifetime."

"And I missed it," she said, pouting.

It was such an uncharacteristic look for her, Finley couldn't help but laugh. He reached forward, gathering her in his arms and pulling her close so she was straddled over his lap, her body pressed against his.

"For you, princess, I'll make an exception and repeat it. Are you paying attention this time?"

She curled her arms around his neck, eyes bright as she whispered, "Yes."

"Then this I swear to you, Quinn Satori. I will protect you from every threat, real or imaginary. From this day forward, it's my life for yours. No matter the cost."

Tears pricked her eyes as she swallowed. "Who knew Guardians were so swoony?"

He smiled, ignoring her comment as he asked, "Do you know it means, my giving you my vow?"

She bit her bottom lip and shook her head, her gaze still intent on his.

"It means that I'm bound to you, Quinn. Forever. Nothing—not even a too stubborn for her own good memory weaver—will ever be able to come between us. So you see, I couldn't leave you now if I wanted to. You never need to worry about it again, not even in your dreams."

Her soft gasp washed over him as the tears she'd been fighting spilled down her cheeks.

He wiped them away with the pads of his thumbs, whispering, "I'm yours, Satori. From this moment until I take my final breath, I will always be yours."

# EPILOGUE
## QUINN

*— One Year Later —*

Quinn waved goodbye to Greta, the masseuse Finley surprised her with that morning. Four glorious hours later, she'd been pampered to within an inch of her life. Truth be told, she'd have much rather it been his strong, oiled-up hands rubbing down the length of her naked body, but she was smart enough not to say so. It might ruin the surprise.

Finley was up to something—he'd been scheming for weeks—and today, finally, she was going to find out what he'd been up to. Or that's what she assumed since it had been one year to the day since Finley had given her his vow. That had to be significant, right?

Her eyes narrowed as she tightened the belt of her satin robe.

Unless he'd forgotten.

In which case, no blow jobs for Batman. She wouldn't give him so much as a striptease. He'd be cut off, cold turkey. A complete sex embargo. Too bad, so sad, he and his blue balls could just commiserate in silence until they made appropriate amends for forgetting such a momentous occasion.

She laughed at her bravado. There was absolutely no way that would fly. Finley had an entire year's experience under his belt when it came to manipulating her body. He'd have her caving in an hour, tops. The sexy bastard.

If she'd learned anything in their year together, it was that she was absolute putty in his hands. One growled command, or hell, even a single searing look, and her body was obeying before her brain even realized what it had agreed to. Such was his power over her.

And she wouldn't trade it for anything.

It was the mother of all miracles, but there you had it. Fierce, independent, head bitch in charge Quinn Satori absolutely loved being owned. She'd blossomed under Finley's tender care, his unfailing patience, strength, and dominance softening her sharp edges. Well, most of them. She was still the same badass babe she'd always been, just now with a new and improved outlook on life.

Finley had shown her what it meant to be loved, to belong heart and soul to another. She realized now the years she'd spent denying what existed between them had been little more than a half-life. It wasn't until she'd dared to take the leap and put her happiness in his very capable hands that she truly understood what it meant to be alive.

That wasn't to say it was all sunshine and rainbows. She still had the nightmares, though they came less and less frequently these days. Most of the time, Finley holding her close and reminding her of his vow was enough to break her free of its hold. But other times, when it wasn't enough to send the darkness scattering, he'd take control of her body by welding pleasure and its twin pain so expertly her mind was forced into blissful submission. He knew exactly what she needed, mastering her completely in those moments until the only thing she could focus on was him.

Quinn had never been happier or more in love. Which was why she knew, she just *knew*, he had something special up his sleeve for today. Her Batman wouldn't dare let her down.

Following the soft strains of the piano, Quinn padded down the hall toward the back of the penthouse. Even though she'd heard the music, she hadn't been expecting the scene waiting for her in the living room. Finley sat at the piano, his hair disheveled, his white shirt unbuttoned, the sleeves rolled up, his hands gliding over the keys. She didn't even know he could play; she'd always assumed the instrument was some kind of billionaire showpiece.

*"Get your sweet arse over here, Satori."*

Already turned on by the proof of his mastery of the piano, the rough timbre of his voice in her mind sent her desire for him through the roof. He hadn't even needed to look up to know she was there. It made his gruff command even sexier.

*"I'm enjoying the show."*

He pinned her with his gaze, his eyes unerringly finding hers across the room. *"Don't make me tell you again, princess."*

*"Well, somebody's in a mood."*

*"Somebody's been waiting four bloody hours for a kiss."*

*"And whose fault is that?"*

*"Yours."*

*"You're the one who sent me off for a spa day as soon as my eyes opened."*

*"There's always time for a proper good morning."*

*"I'll try and remember that next time."*

*"Get over here, sweetheart, and make it up to me now."*

Quinn bit back her laugh as she slowly made her way across the living room, loving the way his eyes tracked her progress and how he never missed a single note as he continued to play.

Mirth shone in his hazel eyes, along with the hot blaze of arousal as she rounded the corner of the instrument, stopping beside the bench. *"That's some dress you're wearing, princess. Take it off."*

Lust detonated inside her, pure and potent. She couldn't resist teasing him a little, knowing he'd make her pay for it, and looking forward to the punishment. *"It's not a dress, it's a robe."*

*"It's lovely. Now take. It. Off."*

*"I'd rather you take it off."*

His eyebrow quirked up. "Is that so?" he asked aloud, his hands finally going still on the ivory and black keys.

She lifted a shoulder, the silky amethyst sliding down. "It's more fun that way."

He twisted so smoothly, she wasn't even aware he'd moved until his hands were already around her hips and lifting her up. A breathless giggle escaped as he set her down on the keys, a loud discordant trill echoing around the room as he did.

"Well, that's one way to make music."

He grinned at her. "Where's my kiss, Satori?"

She leaned forward, wrapping her arms around his shoulders and settling her feet more firmly on either side of his hips on the bench. "Right here, handsome. Waiting for you to take it."

His hand was in her hair and pulling her forward before she finished speaking. His lips were warm and soft beneath hers, the kiss slow and languid. Like they had all the time in the world to savor each other.

She'd just slid one of her hands down the back of his shirt so she could rake her nails over his spine the way he loved when he pulled back, giving her bottom lip a soft nip. "I have something for you."

"Oh? Tell me I get to unwrap it," she whispered, shifting so she could reach down and cup the straining length of his erection.

His laughter was a quiet rumble. "That's not what I was referring to."

"Pity. It's my favorite."

"Be a good girl, and maybe you'll get that too."

Warmth spread through her chest and moved down to her core, just like it always did when he said those two words. Unable to help herself, she brushed her lips over his, her voice a sultry whisper, "Okay, Daddy."

He growled. "Behave, minx. I'm trying to give you a present."

"Then give it to me already."

There was no mistaking the innuendo in her breathy demand.

His eyes sparked with sexual fire as they held hers. "Oh, I intend to."

"Well then, what are you waiting for?"

"I gave you an order you've yet to obey." Her confusion must have registered on her face because he gave the belt of her robe a sharp tug, untying it.

*Right.*

With all the kissing and the teasing, she'd forgotten he wanted her naked.

He moved his hands until his palms rested on her knees, his thumbs skating over the exposed skin of her inner thighs.

"Are you wearing anything under that robe, Satori?"

Her lips curled with mischievous invitation, recognizing Finley's game. "Maybe."

He pushed her knees wider. "Prove it."

Instead of sliding off the robe like he wanted, she inched the fabric up her legs, using her fingers to reel the satin back like a curtain. Legs spread as they were, there was no way to hide her body's obvious reaction to him. His eyes dropped down, nostrils flaring as he sucked in a breath.

"Already so fucking wet for me," he whispered, his hungry gaze lifting back to meet hers. "Now the top."

He didn't need proof of her nudity beneath her robe. Her nipples were tightly pebbled and begging for his attention. But then, this game had never really been about proof.

Movements slow and just as deliberate, she grasped the edge of the cloth and peeled it back, baring one of her breasts as the fabric slid down her arm.

He hummed approvingly low in his throat. "Have I told you how fucking gorgeous you are, Satori?"

"Not today."

He leaned forward, taking one straining bud in his mouth and sucking. Hard. Then he scraped his stubbled jaw along the inner curve of her breast, his voice floating up to her.

"The gods themselves are jealous of your beauty. They'd steal you from me, if they could, just to be near it."

"Flattery will get you everything, darling."

"I already have everything, princess. I have you."

"Fin . . ."

She'd been so distracted by his mouth trailing kisses along her chest, she hadn't noticed when he reached behind him to pick up a flat velvet box. Giving her an almost boyish grin, he held it out to her. "Happy Anniversary."

She blinked a couple of times, her brain feeling fuzzy with arousal. "Why get me all riled up if you're just going to do a bait and switch?"

"Because I want this to be the only thing you're wearing when I slide inside you."

"Oh."

Pulse racing, Quinn reached out and took the blue box from him. Giving him one last curious look, she lifted the top. Her breath caught as she spotted the exquisite piece of jewelry nestled in its bed of cream-colored satin.

"Fin," she breathed, carefully picking up the delicate platinum choker.

The black diamond-encrusted bat, no bigger than her fingernail, threw rainbows on the wall as the tiny stones caught and reflected the light streaming in from the window behind her.

"It's beautiful."

"I wanted you to have something that marked you as mine."

She forced herself to look up, a sheen of tears blurring his face as she let out a watery laugh. "Okay, caveman. You've been spending too much time with Nord. Was weaving our essence together not permanent enough for you?"

His lips hitched. "No one else can see that. Jewelry requires less of an explanation."

She was searching for a clasp, eager to feel it resting against her skin. His hand wrapped over hers, taking the necklace from her.

"There's no clasp. It's not meant to come off," he explained, likely skimming the unvoiced question from her mind.

"Then how—"

But she should have known.

His eyes blazed silver as he separated the small pendant from the chain and then settled it around her throat. With a second, final display of magic, he sealed the choker closed. That's when his words clicked. It wasn't just a choker; it was a *collar*.

A small tremor worked its way through her hand as she rested her fingertips over the tiny bat. "Fin, is this . . ."

She couldn't finish the question, afraid she might be reading too much into a single piece of jewelry.

He cupped her cheeks, thumbs brushing away the stray tears that had slipped free. "I wanted to give you something that felt more like us, but if you'd prefer a ring—"

"Finley . . ." she interrupted his nervous ramble, "are you proposing to me?"

He tilted his head, his eyes narrowing. "Isn't it obvious?"

"Uh, no. Usually the guy gets down on one knee, or you know, there's a question involved."

He laughed, the sound warming her heart. "You'll have to forgive me, sweetheart. In my day, betrothals were legal matters hashed out on paper between two aging fathers and, more often, a pair of scheming mothers. I never really gave marriage much of a thought. It seemed like something intended for other people, especially once I joined the Brotherhood. Am I buggering it up completely?"

She couldn't speak around the ball of emotion lodged in her throat, so she shook her head.

"Does that mean you'll be mine, Satori?"

"Silly Batman, I already am."

His smile could have melted her panties had she been wearing any. "Yes, but now everyone else will know it too."

He kissed her then, laying claim to her body the same way he had her heart. And it was just like she suspected. Finley would never, not even once, let her down.

*— A Few Years Later —*

"That's it, sweetheart. Come for me."

Finley's hand tightened in her hair and gave a sharp tug, pulling her torso up and off the hood of the black Bugatti. Once her back was pressed to his chest, the hand fisting her hair moved to wrap around her throat, and the other dipped between her legs.

Her thighs were still trembling from the force of her last orgasm, the second he'd given her since he'd bent her over his prized possession and started fucking her like he was born to do it.

"I can't," she moaned, even as the fingers working her clit sent her spiraling.

His mouth was at her ear, his lips as responsible for the shivers racing down her body as his rough whisper. "You can and you will, princess. Come for Daddy."

"Jesus fuck, Fin."

He laughed, and the vibration of his chuckle, along with his relentless thrusts and skilled fingers, sent her straight over the edge.

"Fuck I love the way you squeeze my cock when you come," he growled, sinking his teeth into the back of her neck as the pumps of his hips turned brutal.

She loved when he lost control like this, finally allowing himself to chase his own pleasure. He was holding nothing back, slamming into her so hard she knew she'd feel the imprint of him for days after. And that she'd likely sport bruises on her hips from being rammed into the hood of the car.

Worth it. So fucking worth it.

Especially when she'd finally convinced him to make this particular fantasy come true. And on the Bugatti of all vehicles. His stable had multiplied quickly in the last few years, but his Batmobile was still the crown jewel of his collection.

And her personal favorite, especially now that her handprints were quite literally all over it.

He finished with a grunt, whispering kisses along her neck as he held her tight. She could still feel his cock twitching inside of her. She loved this part too. When their hearts were racing and their breath still uneven, but the world was silent except for the two of them existing in their own blissed-out bubble.

Finley pulled out of her, and she could feel him dripping down her thigh. He made a contented sound.

"Leave it," he ordered, slapping her on the ass. "I want to know you're still dripping with my cum while I'm forced to mingle with a bunch of surly Vikings."

She looked at him over her shoulder. "You really want me walking around a party leaking your cum."

He winked, looking pleased with himself. "Yup."

"You're a savage."

"You love it."

"Fuck me, but I do."

He tucked himself back into his pants and zipped up, managing to look like his billionaire alter ego once more. She knew she wouldn't be as lucky. No matter what she did, she was going to look well fucked, and Lina would know exactly why they were running an hour late to her sons' birthday party, so she didn't bother to do more than straighten her clothes. She pulled down her skirt, which Finley had left bunched up her waist, and then snagged her shirt off the floor next to the forgotten blanket.

"I'm surprised you didn't insist on the blanket," she murmured, fluffing her hair and then fishing her lipstick out of her purse, which had also been tossed on the floor.

He looked at her and then at the his and hers handprints on the car.

"Worth it."

"Really?"

"Oh yeah, princess. I've been dreaming about that for years."

The look on his face was enough to have her clenching her thighs. "Fuck, Batman. You keep looking at me like that we'll never make it to the party."

"Yes, we will. It's only a portal away."

He reached for her, this time lifting her up and setting her on top of the car.

"Fin," she protested, but it was halfhearted at best.

"Shh," he said, pushing her back and spreading her legs. "Be my good girl and give me one more for the road."

*— An hour later, in Novasgard —*

"I can't believe Alek and Tor are already seven."

Lina gave her a look filled with exasperation. "You're telling me. It would have been easier keeping track of the twins' birthday if they were Leap Year Day babies. Who thought raising them in two different realms was a good idea?"

"I believe that was you," Nord said, smiling indulgently at his wife.

"Yeah, well, when I wanted them to learn about the other half of their heritage, I didn't consider having to keep track of two separate timelines."

"Is that why you decided to stick to Novasgard once Astrid was born?" Quinn asked.

Lina's expression went soft as her eyes fell to the daughter cuddled in Nord's arms. "Yes."

Quinn had already asked several times to hold her new

goddaughter, but the berserker refused to part with her. She was barely a month old and already had her father wrapped around her sweet little finger.

"You should see him with the boys," Lina whispered. "Before Astrid was born, he would sit them down and explain the importance of being a big brother. Of how it was their duty to care for and protect her. It turned into a nightly ritual. I've never seen those two sit still for anything that wasn't related to weapons or food, but they ate that shit right up."

Quinn laughed. "That poor angel is going to have a rough time of it when she starts dating. With two berserkers for parents and a couple of badasses in training for brothers, her future suitors don't stand a chance."

"Like you're going to be any better."

Her answering grin could have cut glass. "Oh, I will be the worst of the lot. Anyone tries to fuck with my godkids, and I will ruin them."

Baby Astrid squealed with approval. Or that's how Quinn translated the gurgling sounds coming from the bundle in Nord's arms. She shook her head, finding it nearly impossible to reconcile the man cooing to his daughter in Norse with the one she remembered nearly tearing a house down with his bare hands.

"Well, that's it. You did the impossible. You tamed a beast."

Lina laughed. "I think that little girl has more to do with it than me. But you're not wrong. He's completely domesticated these days."

"I'm standing right here."

"Well, am I wrong?"

Nord glanced up at his wife with a grin. "I know better than to answer that."

Lina put her hands on her hips. "Careful, Viking. I know where you sleep."

"Peace, Kærasta. I meant no offense."

"Uh huh," she murmured, eyes narrowed playfully as he leaned down to steal a kiss.

"I'm going to lay her down for her nap. Be right back," he promised, heading off in the direction of their house.

"Gods, fatherhood looks good on him. I thought he looked like sex on a stick on a battlefield, but that was before I saw him cuddling a baby," Lina said, fanning her face.

"Does this mean we can look forward to more nieces and nephews?" Finley asked, leaving Cora to come join them.

Lina grimaced, her hand rubbing her lower belly. "Not anytime soon. Pregnancy with Astrid was a totally different ball game than with the twins. Does it make me a bad mother to admit that?"

"Of course not," Quinn said.

"I'm just not in a hurry to repeat the experience. I spent eight out of nine months with my head in the toilet. I'm enjoying the break."

Finley wrapped his arm around her shoulders. "You know you're welcome at the penthouse anytime you need a vacation."

She raised an eyebrow. "And would that include full use of your secret spa?"

"Absolutely."

"Hmm, I might just take you up on that. I have business with Crombie I have to see to in Bell Falls anyway, might as well make a weekend out of it. I've been putting it off for months."

"What is the King of the Cockwombles up to these days?" Finley asked.

"Making friends everywhere he goes from the sound of it."

"And since you're his only friend, clearly you mean enemies," Quinn said.

Lina laughed. "Pretty much. All he said is that he needs my help, some new club owner, Lily, I think her name is, is threatening to ruin his business."

"Uh oh," Quinn said. "Sounds like he might have met his match."

Lina crossed her fingers. "One can only hope. Falling in love is just what our favorite faerie needs. Anyway, what about you two? Any kids in Mr. and Mrs. Satori's future?"

Quinn and Finley grinned at Lina's cheekiness. She loved that

Finley had taken Quinn's name and brought it up every chance she could. It was technically the way of the Satori since they were matri-archal, but it tickled Lina to no end that her alpha male adopted brother hadn't insisted on Quinn taking his.

She'd offered, actually, when they'd signed the documents legally binding them to each other, but Finley had said no. He'd rather take hers since it held importance to her. Especially since he had no ties to his family name, which was St. Aubyn, as it turned out. The Guardian who'd rescued him from the mean streets of London had been none other than his long-lost biological father. He'd apolo-gized on his deathbed, swearing that he would have come for Finley sooner if he'd known the woman he'd had a dalliance with at some society ball had gotten with child.

It was all very dramatic and scandalous, and Quinn thought it absolutely perfect that Finley was the result of a one-night stand from straight out of one of her historical romance novels. It was probably wishful thinking on her part, but she was sure that was the reason he was such a skillful and attentive lover. How could you not be when you were conceived from a night of illicit passion?

Finley wrapped his arms around Quinn's waist, leaning down to press a kiss to her cheek. "No little ones in our immediate future. We're still having fun making up for lost time."

"And I'm not exactly the maternal type."

"Bullshit, I've seen you with the twins. You'd be an amazing mom."

Quinn shrugged. "Well, for now, I'll just spoil your kids and call it a day."

Lina laughed. "I'm just going to ask Cora. I bet she knows."

"Ask me what?" Cora asked, sweeping over to them with a grace Quinn envied.

Her mother barely looked a day over thirty-five. Though Quinn didn't need her gift to know the girlish flush tinging her cheeks was due to the Novasgardian gazing at her from the other side of the yard. Sten had become, if not a boyfriend exactly, definitely her mother's companion. The fisherman was good for her. Warm. Compassionate. Adventurous. He knew how to give her mother the quiet moments, a fact which wasn't lost on either of the Satori women.

Quinn didn't think Cora would ever fall in love again like she had with her first husband, but Quinn was ecstatic she wasn't alone anymore. Especially now that her own days were filled with Animagi business and her nights consumed by Finley.

"Your daughter and son-in-law don't think they'll have children. What about you? What do you see in their future?"

"Oh no," Cora said with a laugh. "You're not getting me in the middle of this one. Some things are best left for fate to reveal when she's ready."

As soon as the words left her lips, Cora's irises started to swirl like lavender smoke.

"Oh crap, now look what you've done," Quinn groaned.

Lina shrugged, looking completely unrepentant. Neither of them were smiling when Cora started speaking.

"Five lives bound together. And one that hangs in the balance. The end begins with him."

"Oh great, here we go again. I thought we were done with this end of the world bullshit," Quinn grumbled.

"No, not you," Cora said, sending ice skittering down her back. "*Him.*"

Her eyes were leveled on the twins, playing happily in the dirt.

Lina lifted a hand to her mouth, her eyes shining too bright in her pale face. "It—it can't be one of them. They're just babies. You must have gotten it wrong."

But Cora was never wrong, and Lina knew it.

Swallowing, looking like she was about to be ill, Lina asked, "Which one of my sons is in danger, Cora?"

The smoke had vanished from Cora's eyes, leaving behind a wary resolution. "I don't know, mon coeur. But I have a feeling we're going to find out sooner rather than later. Destiny has big plans for one of your sons. Prepare them both because when that day comes, whichever one it is will need all the help he can get."

NOT READY TO SAY GOODBYE TO THE UNDERCOVER MAGIC CREW? GOOD NEWS, YOU DON'T HAVE TO!

OBSESSION IS A BRAND-NEW PARANORMAL ROMANCE FEATURING SOME FAMILIAR FACES AND INTRODUCING YOU TO SOME NEW ONES.

KEEP READING TO CHECK OUT THE FIRST CHAPTER OF BOOK 1 IN MY SPICY REVERSE HAREM SERIES, THE MATE GAMES: WAR, CO-WRITTEN WITH K. LORAINE.

# OBSESSION SNEAK PEEK
## CHAPTER 1: THORNE

It was a shame Sunday Fallon had to die tonight. And that I would be the one to kill her. But there was nothing I could do now that I'd caught her scent. Not after two solid days of her existing in my space. Blackthorne Hall was my domain, the place I ruled without question because it bore my family name. Until now, I'd spent the last three years in complete control. Until her.

She called to me. Drew me to her with that irresistible, decadent scent. Made me mad with hunger. Desperate with need. Obsessed.

My father told me stories of how mother had tempted him, how her blood had been like no other. I'd never experienced it until now. I was hunting her. Not because I wanted to. I *had* to. I had to sample this irresistible creature. To know if she could possibly taste as delicious as she smelled.

Each one of her rhythmic footfalls teased me as she jogged through the campus trails, her measured breaths and elevated heartbeat strong in my ears. It took everything in me not to rush to her and sink my fangs into her throat, just as it had each night as she went about her routine. Tonight, I was within arm's reach, ready to take her, but that would mean it was over almost before it began.

The monster in me wanted to draw it out, to savor the chase, because once I had her, that would be it.

She slowed to a walk, hands on her hips as she stared up at the moon and sighed. "This is it. This is what you get for being different. You finished college but still ended up being shipped off to a glorified boarding school for the supernatural's elite to keep you out of trouble."

Her voice was smooth and silky with the barest rasp to it. Music to my ears. If I killed her, I'd never hear it again. Perhaps I'd turn her instead. Make her mine forever. The thought had merit. Except, of course, for the fact that she was the princess of the Fallon wolf pack. Something told me her family would take issue with a Blackthorne vampire draining her dry and then making her one of us. We didn't want to start a war now, did we?

Her sharp intake of breath had me slinking into the shadows as she glanced over her shoulder in the direction where I'd been standing. "Is someone there?"

I smirked. Someone was definitely there. A predator. A hunter. The creature who'd change her life irrevocably.

Not tonight, though. I'd keep myself on the edge of euphoria a little longer. It was more fun that way.

As she rounded the corner, I kept my distance, now following just to ensure my prey returned safely home. I couldn't risk someone else catching her. She was mine. Whether she knew it yet or not. Her dark hair swung back and forth in the high ponytail she wore, the ends brushing her shoulders and calling attention to her slender white neck. I wondered if her skin would change from porcelain to pink when she blushed and her blood rushed to the surface. Instinct took over, lengthening both my cock and my fangs. Arousal pulsed through me, eclipsed only by my hunger. I wanted her with every cell in my body.

"Everything all right there, Thorne?" The Irish lilt of Father Caleb Gallagher's voice stopped me mid-step.

"Priest." I acknowledged him with the barest tilt of my head.

His jaw clenched at the title, a reminder of his past life as a man of God before he'd been turned into one of my kind. "Leave her be, Mr. Blackthorne. She's not for you to toy with."

"My instinct says different."

"Do not think your family name will exempt you from consequences if you kill her. The war—"

I waved my hand. "Yes, I know. The Families are on thin ice as it is, a war will start, death, bloodshed, etcetera." We had shared a relative peace between the head Families of our supernatural kinds the last twenty-five years. Since my father took control of the Blackthorne vampire kingdom and created a sort of treaty with the remaining shifter packs and witch covens. The alliance was nothing short of fragile after our kind spent centuries trying to rule over every preternatural species in existence.

I sighed heavily into the darkness. "No blood was spilled."

He arched one dark brow. "Yet."

"I will keep my distance."

"See that you do. You may be a prince, but I'm still in charge here."

I scoffed. "You're a professor. You have no control over me."

"One call to your father and you'll spend a week in the well. You know as well as I that he won't hesitate to isolate you if you pose a risk to the stability of our world, Noah Blackthorne."

I shrugged, trying to play it cool, but I'd spent two days in the well back home once simply so I'd know to fear it. My father was still ruthless when he needed to be.

"Keep her away from me if you want to ensure she's safe."

"You're hunting her."

I swallowed past a burning throat. Yes, I was. "I can control myself."

"Perhaps she'd be safer living in my quarters until you've found a new distraction."

A low snarl escaped before I could stop myself. The thought of Sunday spending any time in this man's home, sharing his space and his air, made unreasonable jealousy unfurl in my gut. Vampire or not, he was still a priest. A veritable eunuch, castrated by his faith and vow of celibacy. He couldn't have her, even if he wanted her. She was mine to claim.

"She's fine here. We're separated by three floors of concrete. I won't ravish her until she asks for it."

He shoved his hands into the pockets of his dark slacks, a wary expression on his face. "Goodnight, Thorne. Best get behind closed doors before you lose hold of your monster."

I shook my head before turning away and heading off in the direction Sunday had.

Which of the dorms in this hall was hers? My gaze swept over the doors, senses on high alert as I searched for her, but all I smelled now was a mixture of creatures, from vampire to shifter to witch. Until I caught it again as I stepped into my elevator. Sweet and rich with a darkness I couldn't name. Unlike anything else. Sunday Fallon called to me, begged me to claim her. To taste her. I palmed my aching cock as the doors to the top floor opened, and I strode to my suite.

I would have the beautiful little shifter if it was the last thing I did. And it just might be.

DON'T MISS A SECOND OF THIS SUPER SPICY PARANORMAL REVERSE HAREM FEATURING SOME OF YOUR FAVORITE UNDERCOVER MAGIC CHARACTERS! GRAB YOUR COPY OF OBSESSION NOW!

# ALSO BY MEG ANNE

**THE CHOSEN UNIVERSE**

**THE CHOSEN**

*A FATED MATES HIGH FANTASY ROMANCE*

MOTHER OF SHADOWS

REIGN OF ASH

CROWN OF EMBERS

QUEEN OF LIGHT

THE CHOSEN BOXSET #1

THE CHOSEN BOXSET #2

**THE KEEPERS**

*A GUARDIAN/WARD HIGH FANTASY ROMANCE*

THE DREAMER (A KEEPER'S PREQUEL)

THE KEEPERS LEGACY

THE KEEPERS RETRIBUTION

THE KEEPERS VOW

THE KEEPERS BOXSET

**THE FORSAKEN**

*A REJECTED MATES/ENEMIES-TO-LOVERS ROMANTASY*

PRISONER OF STEEL & SHADOW

QUEEN OF WHISPERS & MIST

COURT OF DEATH & DREAMS

# THE MATE GAMES UNIVERSE
## BY K. LORAINE & MEG ANNE

### <u>War</u>

Obsession

Rejection

Possession

Temptation

Devotion

### Pestilence

Promised to the Night (Prequel Novella)

Deal with the Demon

Claimed by the Shifters

Captive of the Night

Lost to the Moon

### <u>Death</u>

Haunting Beauty

Hunted Beast

Hateful Prince

Heartless Villain

<u>**Apocalypse**</u>

Sin

Chaos

Malice

Grim

Lucifer

# MORE BY MEG & KIM

**<u>Twisted Cross Ranch</u>**

*A dark contemporary cowboy reverse harem*

Sinner's Secret

Corruptor's Claim

Deadly Debt

# ABOUT MEG ANNE

USA Today and international bestselling paranormal and fantasy romance author Meg Anne has always had stories running on a loop in her head. They started off as daydreams about how the evil queen (aka Mom) had her slaving away doing chores, and more recently shifted into creating backgrounds about the people stuck beside her during rush hour. The stories have always been there; they were just waiting for her to tell them.

Like any true SoCal native, Meg enjoys staying inside curled up with a good book and her fur babies . . . or maybe that's just her. You can convince Meg to buy just about anything if it's covered in glitter or rhinestones, or make her laugh by sharing your favorite bad joke. She also accepts bribes in the form of baked goods and Mexican food.

Meg is best known for her leading men #MenbyMeg, her inevitable cliffhangers, and making her readers laugh out loud, all of which started with the bestselling Chosen series.